WORKING ME OVERTIME

A Novel By,

ANESHIA SCOTT

Your FACE you would
Look better BETWEEN our pages!

Check us out at
www.afterhourspublications.com

WORKING ME OVERTIME

Chapter 1

The soft keys on the computer clicked away as the sound of the buzzing of people's conversations flooded the quiet office suite. Devan was lost in her transcript that needed to be done to be on her boss', Mr. Jones', desk by 5 p.m. She sighed wearily. It was a humid Friday afternoon around 2 o'clock, and the weekend was here! Sadly, Devan didn't have anything planned. Being new to the Detroit area, and she had just transferred from Atlanta, Ga to get away from her family and a cheating ex-boyfriend of five years.

Devan worked as a secretary for Jones, Jones, and Wallace on the fifteenth floor of the exotic looking high rise building. She loved her job but needed, and craved more excitement. She was a voluptuous size twenty-two with perky size thirty-eight full "D" cups, with an eighteen-inch waist, and a big round smooth feeling ass, that cast attention from men of all color and age. She was thirty-three years old, but can easily pass for twenty-five to twenty-seven on any day. Her mocha brown complexion with almond hair that was kept in a bun during work hours, and cascaded past her neckline for going out or casually chilling at home completed her looks. Devan's condo overlooked Detroit's boisterous city limits, and was adjacent to her job at the firm, so her commute to work wasn't far at all.

I need to get laid, she thought to herself as she finished one folder, placed it in the "done pile" and started on a new one. She sighed again.

Three more hours and I get to go home, put on my sweats, and curl up with a Zane book with my cocoa, she thought sighing again.

"This is my life for now."

She continued typing away stopping momentarily to finish her chamomile green tea, and wave to Sara, the secretary for Mr. Wallace, from across the room. There were three of them, her, Sara, and Tyler who were all secretaries at the prestigious law firm. Tyler had Eric Jones SR, while Devan had Eric Jones Jr. Both senior and junior were both gorgeous as they each stood at 6foot 3 inches in height, cocoa brown skin with dark piercing eyes.

Senior's eyes were, of course, a little older, wiser, in his years with crow's feet. Nevertheless, still a very gorgeous man to look at. Erick Jr. was fine as hell with the same dark features as his father; broad chest with strong arms, and six pack that had women transfixed on him through his clothes. The third partner, Craig Wallace was of mixed race and resembled the actor Robert Townsend off of the 90's show "The Parenthood". He was into white women with black women shapes and was rumored to be fucking Sara.

Occasionally, Craig would flirt with Devan, but her eyes were on Erick Jr. Often Erick Sr. would make passes at her, nothing serious enough to file sexual harassment, just flowers on her desk, or coupons to a salon and a spa for the day. She was flattered, but she never adhered to his advances. She simply thanked him and kept it professional. Besides, Erick Jr. was who she wanted to give her pussy to. She wondered if Eric Jr. was single. He wasn't married, that she knew, but she still wondered. He never let his job and personal life correlate, and thus he remained a mystery. As if on cue, he stepped out of his office walking over to her desk.

"Hey Devan, Devan," he said flashing his smile at her.

"Hmm? Oh sorry, Mr. Jones, " Devan said, snapping out of her mini fantasy of him.

"That's ok hun," Eric chuckled. "Please pause on that transcript and locate this file for me for court tomorrow?" He asked handing her a piece of paper with a bar code on it.

"Sure, I can Mr. Jones," Devan said standing up.

He stepped back as she stood, broadcasting her full-figured frame with her *Vera Wang* white blouse, and charcoal gray pencil skirt. On her feet, she wore her light gray *Marc Jacobs* pumps. Her plump ass bounced in her skirt as she walked away from him. Eric let his eyes roam her body and felt a slight erection in his pants at the mere thought of how good her ass would feel as she straddled his face while snacking on her pussy.

"Damn!" He whispered fixing his tie and clearing his throat as he briskly walked back to his office, hoping the bulge in his pants went unnoticed. Devan neared the corridor, turned left, and went inside the door marked file room. Her heels clicked across the floor as she searched for the file, "**People Versus Augusta**." After locating the file, she shut the lights off, and retreated to her desk. She sighed again, partially eavesdropping on Sara's phone conversation of setting up a date for the night.

Damn how does this bitch do it? She wondered.

Sara giggled and responded to the caller in a hushed tone. Glancing at Devan, she gave her the "thumbs up" sign. Devan downed the rest of her tea. She got up, readjusted her skirt, and walked the short distance to Erick Jr.'s office. She tapped lightly on his door, which was partially open. He waved her in as he finished his phone call.

Shyly, she stood by the door waiting for her turn. Within seconds, he hung up and fixed his attention on her.

She cleared her throat before speaking. "Here is the file you need Eri- um Mr. Jones," she stammered.

He laughed slightly, "Devan you can call me Erick anytime."

"No sir," Devan retorted. "That's unprofessional."

Erick stood and walked slowly towards Devan with his hand outstretched. Devan hastily took two steps back, putting distance between the two.

"Devan. do I make you nervous?" He asked.

"Whaa...what?" Devan stuttered.

"Can I have the file?" He asked.

"Oh, I'm sorry!" she remarked, handing him the file. He looked at her and smiled sexily.

"Thank you, Devan."

"Sure," Devan replied and turned to walk out.

"Oh, um Devan?" Erick called out to her.

"Yes?" Devan turned.

"Do you have plans for tonight? I'd like to take you to dinner?"

"Yes, I do," she replied. "I have a sister coming in from out of town.

"Ok, then, maybe some other time."

"Shoot! Shoot, shoot" Devan mentally kicked herself as she walked back to her desk.

Why did I turn him down? She thought to herself.

Maybe it was his aura that intimidated the hell out of her. Just being in the same room as him made her panties wet. It scared her, but in a curious way. She slumped down in her chair pushing the existing files to the side disgusted with herself. Sara rolled her chair up to Devan's desk and asked if she was ok.

"Yes, I'm fine."

"Ok, let me know when you need to take your break."

"I will, thanks," Devan assured her. She glanced at the clock that read 3:45.

She stared at her computer, letting the screen become a blur as she slipped into a daydream.

....

Devan typed away on the last transcript for the night. She figured she'd pack up the rest and take them home with her for the weekend. Everyone was filing out of the office. Everyone was ready to escape the work week and enjoy their weekend. She waved her hand as they said their goodbyes. Sara called out to her asking if she wanted to have a girls' night but Devan declined. All she wanted to do was get home and wash the day's grime off her body. Alone with her thoughts in the office, Devan continued packing her things to leave as well. She was oblivious to the fact that Erick Jr. was still in his office. She thought he, too, had slipped out heading home.

Erick heard the faint sounds of the computer clicking as he got up and peered out into the reception room. He cast his eyes on Devan as she was getting ready to leave for the evening. He felt the bulge in his pants from earlier. It was a clear reminder to him that he had been with a woman in quite some time since his ex-girlfriend Trish, who had left him for a woman she worked with. He chuckled at that. He knew the sex was good, but to leave him for a woman was ludicrous. Trish's response was that he was too well endowed, and she couldn't handle his massive dick. With Trish being 5'6 and 135lbs, Erick surmised that he needed a big, fine healthy woman like Devan to fulfill his needs.

He shook the imaginary cobwebs out of his head and focused his attention back on Devan. He concentrated on the strand of hair that had escaped her pinned up bun. Her white blouse was of see- through fabric, which allowed him to see her black bra that supported her firm round breasts. He zeroed in on the Chinese tattoo that trailed the base of her neck. He wondered how far it went. He took off his jacket, unloosened his tie, and stood at the entrance of the doorway gazing at Devan lustfully.

As Devan dumped trash into her trash basket, she felt goosebumps on her neck as if someone was watching her. She felt silly because she knew everyone was gone for the day, or so she thought. She smelled a faint aura of cologne as she half turned in her chair to find Erick Jr. eying her with a look of sinfulness. Devan cleared her throat.

"I'm just getting to leave. Is there anything you need?

"Yes, how do you taste Devan?" he questioned.

Devan's eyed widened in surprise at his blunt inquiries.

"Devan," he started, stepping over to her. "I like you, I have for a very long time now. I wouldn't be honest if I didn't share with you how much I want to eat your pussy until you spazz out!"

Fuck! She thought as heat rose to her lower back and neck.

Erick stood in front of her and leaned over her as his lips brushed her ear.

"I don't know if you have a man yet, but I want you, now!!"

He took his tongue and slowly licked from Devan's ear to her neck. He playfully sucked on her neck leaving a passion mark. He continued kissing her nose, forehead, and chin. He brought his lips to hers and sucking on her lower lip, working his way into a full kiss. Devan's breathing became short and rapid, creating heart palpitations as if she had been caught in an act of dishonor.

"Erick," She moaned, stopping him. "What if we get caught?"

Erick replied while unbuttoning her top, "That's the thrill of it all!"

His hands felt like an octopus as they slid off her shirt, caressing her back and breasts. He stepped closer and took off his clothes, setting them in a pile at his feet. He revealed his mocha chest that Devan had many nights ago only dreamed of. He had a six pack, rippled with muscles, sexy arms, and a strong back. She leaned back in her seat, biting on her lower lip as Erick took off his boxers freeing his Python.

It was so beautiful, all ten inches of him! Devan let out a guttural moan as she watched Erick's dick grow in size. It pulsated while he stroked his dick up and down slowly as he gazed at her freshly shaved, fat pussy. She sat up again to lean forward to stroke his massive tool. Her hands could barely fit around his girth. She was mentally preparing herself to fit all of him in her mouth. She leaned in and planted her lip gloss covered lips on the head of his dick and blew on it, which made Erick quiver. She swallowed his whole dick, sucking and slurping on his chocolate bar. He closed his eyes in enjoyment gently grabbing Devan's hair. He mouth fucked her while he cupped her left breast, squeezing and pinching her nipple.

Devan continued to suck his dick while massaging his balls. She let her spit drip down his dick all the while enjoying the stare down between each other. Erick bit down on his lip before he began telling Devan how sexy she looked with his cock in her mouth. She moaned in pleasure that she was pleasing him.

Finally, he freed his dick from Devan's mouth, helped her to stand up, and turned her around, so her back was facing him. Her pussy got wetter as she felt Erick's dick throb against her ass, anticipating what was coming next. He cupped her breasts trailing kisses from her neck, shoulders, and back to where her tattoo rested He pulled up her tight pencil skirt until it reached her ass where he bit on it, groping and squeezing.

Devan was hot and ready bracing herself for Erick to stretch her walls with his big dick, but she was in for a surprise unknown to her. Erick took his finger, slid her black thong to the center of her ass, and snatched it off as Devan gasped in surprise. She moaned in pure ecstasy as Erick bent Devan over the chair, spread her ass cheeks, and licked the center of her peach. He stuck a finger in her pussy as he finger fucked her into oblivion.

Erick slowly licked her clit to her asshole and back again. He speed up, making a musical beat with his long tongue. Devan spread her leg wider and bent further over the chair. She enjoyed Erick feasting on her love cave. She closed her eyes as she backed her ass into his face, riding his tongue as he drove it deeper inside of her. Devan's leg bucked slightly as her clit swelled and throbbed while Erick snacked on her. Only the sounds of her juicy pussy and moans filled the office space along with their body heat beginning to rise.

Just as Devan felt that Erick was going to bring her to an orgasm, he suddenly grabbed her ass, waist, and legs turning her upside down, so her pussy was in his face. Erick dove in her pussy further. Spreading her lips wider and using his tongue like a dick, he fucked her insides. Devan let out a scream and moan as she hung upside down. She grabbed his dick, putting it back into her mouth to feverishly suck and lick as if that was her last meal.

She was in awe as to how in the hell Erick was able to pick her up? She centered her mind back to the fuck fest that was going on as they continued feasting on each other. Erick sucked and slurped on her, stopping only to lick around her asshole, giving it a little more attention, before going back her pussy. He stuck his finger in her pussy, moistening his finger only to stick it in her ass slowly until he was all the way in.

Devan bucked and moaned. She grabbed his legs tighter. Her pussy throbbed and jumped as Erick picked up speed applying more pressure to her clit. He knew Devan was about to come soon, and he wanted to taste all of her sweet juices. He slid his tongue all around her clit picking up more speed as he hoisted Devan up. He grabbed her tighter as she squirmed about. Devan's clit was throbbing and became harder as Erick sucked and blew on it. She tried to hold in her nut, but she couldn't any longer as she screamed his name and warm liquid gushed out of her into his mouth.

He tightened his lips, slurping all of Devan's juices. She bucked and wiggled to no avail as Erick lapped up her juices making her orgasm again. Devan was trying to catch her breath as he positioned her in the right way, grabbed his swollen dick, and held it still as he placed it against Devan's pussy. Using the head to rub across her clit before he pushed his girth deep inside, she gasped aloud.

"Oh shit!" Devan shouted.

She knew he was big by observation, but to actually feel him in her was way different. Erick held onto her waist. He rocked inside of her before pulling his dick out to glance down at her juices that coated his dick. He moaned as he pushed his dick back into her. This time with a little more force until his balls were touching her pussy. Devan grabbed her breasts and sucked on her right nipple as Erick teased her clit with his thumb. His moving in slowly, but deep thrusts drove Devan insane. Still bent over the chair, Erick spread her ass cheeks to push himself deeper inside. He wanted to fuck her entire soul and leave her limping for days to come.

He picked up speed as Devan shouted, "Deeper, faster!"

Erick happily obliged. It had been so long since he had sex and with a partner that could handle his size. He fully enjoyed dicking down this beautiful woman. Erick bent down licking and biting on Devan's back per her request. He was driving his dick deeper and harder into her. Thrusting as he smacked her ass, he left red passion marks on her cheeks. She moaned as she stuck her finger in her mouth sucking on it. Erick watched as she did this, which made his dick get harder. He was trying his hardest not to cum prematurely, but her pussy was just too good...too wet, and he knew he was going to bitch up in no time.

He pulled out of Devan, turned her around, set her on the edge of the desk, picked her legs into a "V" shape, and drove his dick in for more. She grabbed the heel of her pumps for leverage while he fucked her half crazy. The sight of her breasts bouncing up and down while his meat was in her, was making him want to pull out and shoot his load. Her moans created a song of lust to match his strokes.

Devan had never been fucked this good in her life. She was enjoying every stroke he put on her body. Erick was about to nut, but he wasn't quite ready. He pulled out of Devan, gently moved her out the way, and sat down in the chair coaxing Devan to sit on him. She did so bracing herself for his length to stretch her pussy in a whole new position. She shivered as she straddled Erick. He licked and kissed her lips as he gripped the back of her neck to porn star kiss her in a way that made her pussy even wetter. He took note as he broke the kiss. He licked his lips sexily, and cocked his head to one side.

"Ride this dick," he said, "get you another nut in."

Devan grinned devilishly as she found her rhythm to ride the big "snake." He placed his hands under her thighs to assist her as she bounced up and down on his dick. She threw her head back as he leaned in to take her breast into his mouth. He bit her nipple and licked her areola. Devan pumped faster and faster, stimulating a rise from her clit, preparing for another orgasm. Erick felt the sensation rise to the head of his dick as she rode him. He grunted biting his lip.

"I'm about to cum," he moaned, as Devan picked up in speed until she felt his dick jump in her.

She quickly got off Erick and squatted in front of him, so he can see her shaved pussy. She grabbed his dick and squeezed the head. She stroked it before she put him in her warm mouth. She slurped, gargled, and pushed his dick to the back of her throat. She cupped his balls and massaged them as they hardened. Suddenly, Erick bucked in the chair and slid down slightly as hot cum shot out of him to fill Devan's mouth.

She moaned and stroked his shaft until all of his seed slid down her throat. Devan flicked her thumb across her clit as she sucked and swallowed him up to bring herself to another orgasm as well. Erick was spent. He sat rigid in the chair with his ass muscles clenched together. His glazed over eyes looked down at Devan as she licked his balls and dick clean. She topped him off by biting on his inner thighs and winked up at him. Erick Jones, Jr. had just gave Devan the dick of a lifetime..

"Devan? Devan?"

"Yes?" Devan shouted at bit too loudly as she was snapped back into reality. "Yes?"

She turned around to find Erick Jr. standing by the office door.

"Devan, are you ok? You're sweating," he observed.

Devan touched her forehead with embarrassment. She grabbed a napkin to dab at her face.

"Oh, I'm fine. I'm sorry. I must have been daydreaming."

Chapter 2

Devan

It had been well over a month since I had that raunchy fantasy of my boss Erick Jr, or Mr. Jones. It was so surreal! It felt like the real thing. So much, in fact, I creamed my panties twice. Images of that day came flooding back as I rode the elevator to the fifteenth floor. After Erick's voice snapped me out of that fantasy and back to reality, I had whipped my head in his direction and stared at him meekly. Color me embarrassed. If I were a white woman or lighter skinned, he for sure would've seen me turn beet red.

I had jumped up from my desk and ran to the elevator at top speed. I had gone home, which was adjacent to the firm, opened a bottle of pink Moscato, and drunk myself into oblivion. In my drunken stupor, I'd gotten an email from the office about a flood on the sixteenth floor due to a busted pipe in the walls of one of the conference rooms. We were reduced to working from home which in fact, I didn't mind at all. It was back to realit. The reality of the fact I had a sexual conquest of my boss that was three skips and a hop from his office door!

So, here I am, in the elevator, about to start my first day back to the office after the renovations and my nerves are all over the place. Those familiar heart palpitations came in full force as I leaned against the guard rail in the elevator for support. The elevator stopped on the fifteenth floor. I quickly smoothed the hidden wrinkles of my multi colored Royal Rae maxi dress, checked my hair, and lips once more before the door opened. Instant butterflies filled my stomach even though my fantasy lover wasn't here. The mere thought of his closeness could be felt. I exhaled and grabbed my phone. I scrolled down, pretended to check my emails as I stepped out of the elevator in hops that Sara and Tyler weren't in yet.

Of course, they were as Sara cheerfully sang out, "Hey gurl!", as I scurried past.

I gave them a nod of my head and proceeded to my desk. Sighing, I logged into my computer. While I waited for it to boot up and went into the break room to fix myself a cup of joe. Stirring sugar into my cup, I allowed my thoughts to drift back to Erick.

The fact that he was in Switzerland was my only saving grace. I had contemplated drawing up a resignation letter to another firm, or work from home if he was willing to demote me to a lesser job with just cases for the office. However, I knew Erick wouldn't allow that without an explanation of some sort.

What could I tell him? That I wanted to feel his dick in my walls, naked on a bear skin rug in front of a crackling fireplace? I snorted at the thought. Sure, I have seen the way he looks at me, but I don't know the extent of his thoughts about me. Was he willing to compromise his career for a secretary? Hell, a man of his stature could probably have a model girlfriend or perhaps a high powered girlfriend. Not a seventeen dollar an hour wage earner.

I was sick of debating with myself over this infatuation with this man. It had me mentally exhausted, but being the Aquarian that I am, it is my worst trait ever. I feared rejection. It would be an epic fail if I dared to be as bold as my mind was telling me, to just say "fuck it," bare all, tell Erick my intentions only to face his rejection. Not to mention the solidarity of my job after that.

No, no, I'll just have to be mum for now and let whatever card rear its hand. I put my cup to my lips inhaling the hazelnut goodness hoping that today would breeze by. Maybe I'll even check my Monospace and E-Harmony accounts later at home. I should see what's out there, get my mind off of Erick. I felt I was way out of my league with him. Sitting back at my desk, I grabbed the first file and began working. After a few hours, I got up, stretched, and went to refill my cup.

On my way, Mr. Wallace stopped me and told me I was needed in conference room five for a briefing. I nodded my head and hurriedly went to my desk to retrieve my Ipad. I headed towards the conference room. As I walked in, I was accompanied by Sara, Tyler, and Mr.Jones Sr, Ericks's father. Mr. Wallace came in the rear closing the door behind him. Mr. Wallace cleared his throat, said good morning, and began briefing us all about the biggest case that possibly has come across our firm in quite a few weeks.

It was the case of Mob daughter Bella Delucci, who's father was Anthony "Guns" Delucci. She was on trial for killing her husband because he snitched to the FEDS. She was rumored to have shot him. Then left him for dead in the bathtub to dismember his body later. The irony of it all was that Bella was in Cancun at the time of his demise, and was heavily guarded by security. Some speculate her security team acted as accomplices, but no one was talking. So far Ms. Delucci had dropped three million dollars on her bond hearing and representation from Jones, Jones, and Wallace. I typed fast, trying to keep up with Mr. Wallace as he rambled on.

I was so into my work and sipping my coffee, I never noticed the door open and close, until I looked up into the eyes of Erick Jr. Choking on my coffee, I started gasping for air as Sara jumped up to pat me on the back. I grabbed tissues to dab at my blouse. Tyler got up as well. She moved my Ipad out of the way. She assisted Sara with a look of alertness. I excused myself and went to the bathroom as fast as possible as I heard Mr. Wallace asking if I were ok.

"Dammit!" I hissed in the bathroom grabbing more towels. Turning the water on, I was so flustered and confused as to why Erick was even here! What the hell was he doing back here?

Sara breezed in with a smirk on her face as she leaned up against the counter.

"What?" I asked her in an annoyed tone.

She chuckled and sang out "You are in love with that man girl!"

I dismissed her with a wave of my hand, clearly not wanting to entertain her ass.

"Don't start no shit, bitch!" I berated her.

Sara laughed it off, "Oh hell, Y'all need to just fuck and get it over with already."

I shot a murderous look her way and ushered her out of the bathroom. We went back to room five to finish the meeting.

"I apologize," I blurted out as I re-entered the room, avoiding any eye contact.

I stole a quick glance Erick's way when he wasn't looking.

Fuck, I thought.

Erick looked dapper in his all black *Brooks Brothers* three-piece suit with the smokey gray *Stacey Adam's* shoes. He closed the space between us in a few quick steps into my circumference.

"Devan, are you alright?" he asked.

"Yes," I quickly answered, looking down into my lap.

I couldn't dare look into his eyes at that moment. His cologne invaded my nostrils which made my clit instantly throb.

"Well good, then let's finish up this meeting," Mr. Wallace stated.

He turned back to the power point on the board. The meeting commenced for thirty more minutes before we were released back to our daily routine.

I shot out of that room as if it were on fire calling out. When my break came, I rushed toward the elevator. I felt as if the walls were closing in on me. I had to get out of there and quick!

Chapter 3

Devan

The afternoon sky lit up like an inside sauna with its heat permeating every corner. I had to shield my eyes as I crossed the lobby's foyer. I waved to Mr. Santos, the building's doorman, as he held the door open for me. Normally I would stop and engage in conversation with him, but I waltzed right through the double doors as the hot sun kissed my forehead. I breathed a huge sigh of relief as I inhaled the natural outdoor aromas, and exhaled the burden that was built up from being that close to Erick. I must have been looking crazy and flustered because passer-bys slowed their afternoon walk to gawk at me. I pulled out my compact mirror and looked at my reflection. A woman walked up to me and put a loving but firm hand on my shoulder.

"Are you ok sugar?" she asked holding me steady. She guided me to a bench near the water fountain and gestured for me to take a seat.

"Yes ma'am," I assured her smiling weakly.

She looked at me for a minute longer and decided I was well enough to leave me be. I nodded my head in agreement and thanked her as she continued with her day. I glanced over at the food cart and got up to get in line. Normally, I would go out to buy lunch, but today I needed something stronger, and my alcohol was at home. Yes, I was going to buy some cigarettes.

I looked around cautiously as the line moved forward as if my sponsor was gonna jump out at any moment to berate me for even thinking such a thought. I really didn't care. I was going to smoke. I needed back up and fast!! Once I got up to the front, I ordered a pack of *Newports* and a lighter. Packing the box, I pulled one out, lit up, and pulled long and hard. I held it in, savoring the forbidden smoke that I allowed to enter my now, virgin lungs.

The sudden arrival of Erick had blood rushing to my head, which had me light headed, much like this cigarette was doing. I was still frazzled and dazed as I quickly lit up another cigarette. I cursed myself for entertaining this habit once more. I started talking to myself as I tried to decide if I was going to have to resign and find other employment.

I wasn't going to be able to keep my job and continue as his secretary. I wanted him in my bed, making my toes curl, and his tongue licking and sucking every crevice of my body. No man has ever come close to making me feel like a little school girl. I don't know if I liked the feeling. His penetrating stare was enough for me. I felt like he was undressing me with his eyes. If a man ever made love to you with just his stare, I can imagine how his love making would be. Would he have me climbing the wall? If he flicked his tongue across my clit would I nut quick? Or is he the "Ima let you get yours before I get mine first" kind of guy?

I surmised whatever kind of lover Erick was, I was going to not be the same woman afterwards. That had me very, very intrigued. I checked my watch and packed my "cancer sticks" into my bag. Quickly, I sanitized my hands, popped a piece of gum into my mouth, and sprayed on some perfume before heading back inside. I was so against going back in, but I had to go draw up a resignation letter. I figured if I can get through the day, I'd be ok. I could leave thirty minutes early, and that would be it. I figured I would give myself a few days, and put in some resumes for a new job.

Chapter 4

Erick

"Damn," I thought, *Devan, looked so damn beautiful today.*

I guess my sudden, but needed arrival had her going mad. I wanted to go over and help when she started choking, but Tyler and Sara beat me to it. So, I played it cool. I didn't want to upset her any more than I already had. I prided myself on reading body language, and I know Devan was in a state of shock. I wasn't supposed to come back to Detroit for another few weeks, but Anthony Delucci's reps reached out to the firm. He was in a disarray of emotions over his daughter's recent tryst with the law.

She wasn't a stranger to the courts. As a juvenile, Bella's record was expunged. She had gotten into trouble for joining a gang, petty theft as well as other misdemeanor violations. This new ordeal was astronomical, and the firm was representing her.

Popping my knuckles, I casually looked out of the window counting the second Devan had gone out of the building. I wanted to go after her, but I'd give her some time and space, then approach her, later. There was so much I wanted to say to her. I wanted to be with her, smell her womanly scent, let my tongue enter every hole on her body. I wanted to give her this dick in the worst way. I love a BBW, (big, beautiful woman), even though my latest ex-girlfriend Trish wasn't big. She was a size eight, but tall at 5'11, so her weight was proportionate. Tish and I were together for five years until one day she gave me her version of a "Dear John" letter. Yes, she left me for another woman.

At first, I laughed because it was a woman, I mean I am very well endowed, but thinking back she never really wanted to have sex with me some days, and when I did, she complained that I was too "hung," and I was stretching her walls. I thought it was an excuse to fuck another man, that is until she brought the other woman around. Nevertheless, I was done with her and ready to move on. I wanted Devan. I was prepared to have her at any cost. Sure, I wanted to date her, take her out on the town, etc., but I wanted to give her this dick and anything else sexually she wanted me to do to her.

Chapter 5

Devan

Detroits' afternoon sun seemed like it wasn't going to cooperate and give in to some shade, with its heat index of 100. I had come out to get some much-needed air and refresh myself, but now it was time to face the music. Time to go back and finish the job I was hired to do, but with one hidden agenda, to officially resign from Jones, Jones, and Wallace. I felt like I gave it much thought and begrudgingly decided I had to walk away, to save face. Erick invaded my most intimate thoughts at random times. It was becoming too much for me. Even that fantasy I had of him seemed so surreal. I had gone home and masturbated and had the biggest orgasm ever! Gathering up some strength, I got up and walked back into the building pressing the UP button for the fifteenth floor. I looked at my phone as it vibrated.

My mom was calling me. Sending her to voicemail, I made a mental note to call her once I got home. My dear mother Patricia was a sweet lady, but she was a talker! Sighing, I stepped off the elevator for the second time today heading to my desk. I could hear my email icon notification going off as I neared my chair. I looked up and in Sara's direction as I clicked on an I.M. from her.

"What's up with you?"

ME: "Yes girl, I am. I just needed to make a phone call. Thanks," I wrote back.

She then sent me a "thumbs up" emoji back.

I clicked out of my email and into the firm's account to log in. I looked over at the clock that read 2:30. I was not going to take a late lunch, but I would work through and leave. Looking over my shoulder, I saw Erick's door was ajar, and he was in a conversation. I looked over at Sara and Tyler's area where they were gossiping as usual, probably about me, who cares. Squaring my shoulders, I clicked on Microsoft with the firm's company logo heading and started typing out my resignation letter. Once I was done, I carefully looked around before hitting the print button, and waited for the two-page document to print out. I was careful to jot down that I was "seeking better employment" as my sole reason for disengaging from the firm.

I was a good employee ever since coming to work for this company. No write ups or tardiness, no unnecessary drama, or fraternization was I involved in. I even carefully spent money from the "petty cash" lock box that we all had in our desks. That cash was used for slight emergencies, cab fare, thoughtful gifts, and cards for our clients after a successful case, so I felt that my resignation will be willingly approved. That is if Erick would approve without digging too deep as to why I want to leave.

This is why after I grabbed the papers from the printer, I folded the letter into an envelope and set it aside until I got ready to leave. I felt somewhat better, yet apprehensive at what I'd done. I had enough money for a few months of bills until I was gainfully employed once again, so I wasn't too worried. I secretly cleaned the contents off my desk as I got prepared to leave. I wanted a clean get away to prevent inquiring minds in my business and to walk out with some dignity.

Fifteen minutes went by. Once I saw Erick go into a room to consult with his father and Mr. Wallace, which is something they do all the time in the early evenings to debrief the day's events, I took that opportunity to take the letter out, place it in front of my desk, shut off my computer, and gathered my bags to leave.

"Hey, Devan you already leaving for the day?" Sara asked rhetorically.

I inwardly groaned as I answered, "Yes, I have a previous engagement, so I'll see you later," I responded, waving my hand at her and Tyler.

I began walking quickly towards the elevators.

"Ok," Sara remarked, "See you tomorrow."

I didn't even respond as the doors closed, drowning out her voice. She will definitely not see me tomorrow. Walking past Mr. Santos again as I strolled toward the doors to exit the building, I smiled at him. Turning to the left, I walked to the corner waited for the traffic light to change to green. When I reached my tenth-floor condo suite, I began to feel weary about quitting my job.

I had to keep telling myself it was for the best. As I entered my building, I stopped in the hallway to check my mailbox. Sticking the key in the key slot, I took the mail out and locked the door back. I turned and called out to my neighbor, Mrs. Peterson, to hold the elevator as I sprinted over to get inside. I smiled at her as we rode the floors until she got off on the eighth floor. Exhaling, I continued to the tenth. I got off and walked the short distance to my door. Once inside, I kicked off my heels, and started my bath water. Turning on the news, I saw the meteorologist calling for evening thunderstorms.

"Damn I'm glad I left when I did," I mumbled.

Once my bath was drawn, and I put some *Ellen Tracy* bath salts in the tub. I took off my clothes, pinned my hair up, and sunk into the hot claw foot tub. Once my bath was done, I got out, dried off, and slipped on my robe. I pulled the sheets back from my California king size bed. I got a chilled bottle of Moscato from the fridge and a wine glass. I pulled the living room drapes closed, clicked off the T.V., and went to my room.

It was a long day. All I wanted to do was just to unwind and drink. I turned on my sound wave stereo, and *Elle Varners* "Refill" crooned in the background. Sighing, I leaned back against my pillows, taking another sip of wine. I imagined Erick lying next to me while he talked sexily in my ear. Or him massaging my toes and then sucking on them. I shuddered thinking about sex with him. I bet he was a beast in the bedroom. I loved a dominate male when it came to hair pulling, ass smacking, and all that.

I set my wine glass on the night table next to me and opened my robe. I took my finger on my right hand, licked it, and started rubbing my clit. I stuck my finger in my pussy, rotating it in, and out as I gasped. My left hand cupped my breast, pinching my nipple as I simultaneously rubbed my clit back and forth to create friction.

I imagined Erick's tongue flicking across my clit, tasting my bud as it hardened. I moaned sexily, mouthing his name as if he could hear me. I imagined his baritone voice telling me how he was going to fuck me, and all the positions he was going to put me in. I started grinding against my fingers pushing them deeper in my hole. I was nearing my orgasm, and I began to feel hot all over. My breathing labored, and I panted as if I were a dog that needed water. I tossed my head from left to right and sunk further into the pillows. I spread my legs far apart and bucked as a tingling sensation filled my lower extremities. I came all over my hand. I let out a guttural moan as my fingers continued working another orgasm out of my body.

"Oh shit! Pssssss!" I shouted as I came again.

I fell back rigid against my sheets counting the seconds until my breathing became normal again. After a few seconds, I leaned over and got the baby wipes out of the drawer to clean myself up. I dimmed the lights just as I heard thunder and heavy rain began to pour down. Nights like this a warm body would have been appreciated, but I took what I could at the moment as I drifted off to sleep listening to the rain.

Chapter 6

Erick

After the briefing on the Delucci case, I retreated back to my office to gather myself and return calls before our daily debriefing with pops and Mr. Wallace. Settling down in my oversized office chair, I looked out into the front office where the secretaries worked. Devan had not yet returned after rushing out earlier. I wanted to go after her, but I felt that she needed a moment. My thoughts drifted back to her situation. Since working for me, I've never seen her with a male companion, even when we hosted our annual picnics or galas. She was a quiet woman, yet loquacious when she needed to be.

I loved that about her. I also loved her thick frame and delicious round ass that hugged every skirt and pant set she would wear. Her perfect round breasts filled out her tops and glistened with whatever lotion or oil she used. I felt my cock begin to throb at the thought of dicking her down over my desk.

Damn! That woman did something to me every time I thought of her. I had looked forward to seeing her once my plane had landed. I was banking on having lunch with her to discuss "work" when I really wanted to discuss us and how much I wanted her in my bed, on my counter tops, on my balcony, and everywhere she would have me. As a Man, my patient nature allowed her time, but my high sex drive wanted to skip all pleasantries, dive in her pussy, and fuck her while sucking all the energy out of her. To me, she's my perfect fit. I was counting down the moments to tell her how I felt, only because I know she felt the same.

My pops knocked on the door, alerting me of our afternoon meeting. I nodded my head as I fixed my erection, and headed to the next room. When the meeting wrapped up, Mr. Wallace excused himself and left. My pops turned to me with an amused look.

"What?" I asked

"Is she that much of a tasty distraction son?" he inquired.

Looking up from my phone, I stared into those identical eyes that I owned.

"That and much more," I replied.

"Well, I suggest you let it be known then. It's not like you don't know her. Now that your feelings for her have intensified, please tell her. After all, she is a beautiful woman".

I agreed with my pops. Yes, Devan and I would be a perfect fit, like a hand and a glove. I didn't want to waste any more time not letting her know how I felt.

"Well," my pops started, "When you two become an item, will she continue working here?"

"Why not?" I stated. "Look at Craig and Sara's thing they have going on," referring to Sara who works for Mr. Wallace. She was a beauty that looked like Angelina Jolie with a body like Paula Patton.

"Well son, do what you have to do. I love Devan. She's a hard worker, a smart girl, and you two seemed fond of each other. I just hope that it won't cause problems if it doesn't work out", he remarked as he patted me on the shoulder.

"It won't pops, it won't," I assured him.

I sat a moment and mulled over my conversation with my father. I mean, why would it be bad? Devan has feelings for me as I do for her. Nothing will go awry, will it? Returning to my office, I saw that Devan had come back in. Sighing, I grabbed some folders to finish up some work. I had plans for Devan, and I couldn't wait.

Chapter 7

Erick

I sat up, stretched, and grabbed my water. Glancing at the clock that read 3:30, I was through for the day, and was about to leave after cleaning off my desk. I was very organized. I liked a clean desk when I left. I looked out and didn't see Devan.

Maybe she went for a late lunch, I thought.

I was going to call her and ask her to dinner at Ruth Chris' Steakhouse. Then, I'd ease into the impending convo that I was dying to get out. Four o'clock on the nose came. As I was about to tap out for the day, a knock sounded on my door, and Sara appeared.

"Yes, Sara? Come in," I welcomed her.

She pushed the door in further and handed me a manila envelope with my name on it.

"Mr. Jones, I was passing by Devan's desk and saw this. I thought I'd bring it to you".

"Thank you, Sara," I said.

Opening up to the contents inside. My brows furrowed as I read her resignation before my eyes.

"What the hell?" I hissed aloud, pinching the bridge of my nose.

I knew I had to leave and talk to her today. I couldn't have her up and leaving me. I folded the paper and put it into my coat pocket. Shutting off my computer, I grabbed my trench coat and umbrella. I couldn't get to the elevator fast enough. Devan had some explaining to do.

Once I got out of the elevator, the rain was coming down hard. Even though her condo was across the street, I decided to go the building's bar that was down the hall from the lobby. It was happy hour, and I needed a drink bad. I accepted the *Paul Masson* the pretty bartender gave me and downed it. She then poured another. I sat nursing my drink. I was pacing myself and giving Devan time to get situated before going to her place.

Brushing the sudden nerve aside that I developed, I paid my tab, gathered my things, and headed out into the rain. Looking up as the rain fell violently from the sky, a gray blanket of fog enveloped the streets as I trudged on. I was on a mission. I hoped the evening would be one to remember. Entering Devan's building, I shook off the excess rain, stomping my feet as I waited for the elevator to the tenth floor. Shoving some peppermints in my mouth, I looked in the mirror and exhaled. I stepped off the elevator, and I made my way to suite 1023.

I took a few minutes to gather myself as I pulled the paper from my pocket. I was here. No going back. Standing in front of the door, I exhaled a few times to gather enough courage before I knocked.

Chapter 8

Devan

The annoying buzzing sound of my alarm clock jarred me from my sleep. I groaned because I forget to turn it off. I can't help it, I'm so militant at times, and I actually time my sleep. I reached up to shut the sound off and turned to watch the rain and thunder paint my outside windows. Glancing at the clock, it was only 8:15. I thought it was later. I willed myself to get up and get something to drink from the kitchen. I swung my legs to the side and shuffled down the hallway.

As I leaned against the counter drinking a sprite, I thought about my actions from earlier. Whenever Erick does find it, I hope he doesn't get too pissed. I'm so infatuated with that man, masturbating to his face made me hot from embarrassment. I can only imagine the things he would do to my body. I was hoping to one day say, 'screw it,' and just tell him how I feel and let the chips fall where they may. What did I have to lose? I mean besides my job. I can always work somewhere eles. I just had to let him know how I truly felt because I was a horny bitch and needed some love.

Pandora was still playing in the background, and I could hear Keith Sweat crooning his song *"Twisted."* That's exactly how I felt, twisted over Erick while I imagined love-fucking him in the rain, in the tub, on the couch, against the wall, or anywhere I could get it. Can you tell I haven't had any in a while?

Turning to head out the kitchen, I passed the door and swore I heard knocking. I paused because I don't know many people here yet, so I don't get many visits unless it was a neighbor to borrow something or another. I continued down the hall until I heard the sound again. Pivoting, I walked back towards the door and looked through the peep hole.

"Oh shit!" I shrieked and slid to the floor.

What the hell was he doing here? The knocking continued as Erick on the other side calling my name.

"J...just a minute please," I managed to get out trying to contain the palpitations of my heart.

Erick was at my door. Oh hell, what the hell?! I stood up, adjusted my robe, unlatched the locks, and disabled the alarm before opening the door. As I pulled the door open, I was assaulted by his cologne and a sweet smell of peppermint. He greeted me with a smile. God this man was fine! He was slightly wet from the rain as he leaned up against the door towering over me.

"Aren't you going to invite me in?" He asked just as my gaze left his face and focused on the letter in his hand.

He was holding my resignation letter.

Chapter 9

Devan

"Um, y..yes," I stammered, "Come in please."

I stepped aside as Erick walked in and stopped as I closed the door. I was unsure of what to say, seeing the letter in his hand.

"Let me take your coat, and I'll go get you a towel to dry off with," I told him as I darted down the hall to my room.

I snatched off my robe. Quickly, I threw on a gray cami and black leggings. I grabbed a towel from the hall closet. I walked slowly up front to find Erick was still in the same spot looking at my living room decor and pictures.

"Here," I offered as I handed him the towel and hung his coat over the tub to dry.

"Thank you, Devan," Erick replied as he dried off.

I bit my lower lip as I watched him roll up his sleeves and wipe his face.

"May I offer you something to drink Eri-um, Mr. Jones?" I asked.

"Yes, please. I'll take some Hennessey, if you have it. Please, call me Erick," he pressed as his eyes stared into mine.

I crossed the room and filled his drink order as he took a seat on the sectional. I was truly in awe to be this close to him, but I didn't want to discuss my reason for leaving the firm. I sat down on the love seat across from Erick and waited for the interrogation to begin.

"You have a nice place, Devan."

"Thank you," I replied.

Taking a sip of his drink, he looked at me for a few moments. I fidgeted in my seat waiting for him to say something-ANYTHING.

"Devan," he began, "I was a bit concerned when Sara brought me your letter that was on your desk this afternoon."

That bitch!, I thought, *Sara is always in somebody's damn business.*

Erick continued, "I don't know why you felt you had to quit. Just take a few days off, or whatever it is you're trying to do, but I just cannot let you leave."

I looked at him in a confused way, but I decided to let him continue.

"Devan, this is hard for me to say, but I'm here now, and I have just to get it out." Erick paused and finished his drink setting the glass down. "I like you, and you know I do. Not only do I like you as an employee, but I've been sexually attracted to you from day one."

"Excuse me a moment," I blurted, grabbing his glass to refill his drink.

As I got to the mini bar, I fixed myself a strong drink and gulped it down, then fixed another. Erick just revealed his feelings for me. I was shocked, happy, but shocked. Crossing the room, I handed him his glass and sat down looking at the floor. I looked up to see Erick staring at me over the rim of his glass.

"Devan, I want you, all of you, if you will have me. I can't tell you how long I have wanted to say that to you", he admitted.

Sipping my drink, I was a little buzzed. I tried to form the words to say to him. He had me very hot, bothered, and speechless. Getting this opportunity again may not be available, so I spoke up.

"Erick, um, I have wanted to tell you how I felt for a while as well. I just didn't want to mix business with pleasure. That's why I wrote that letter. Focusing on work and you is a bit much for me."

"So, what now Devan?" he asked, "Now what? Do you want me, because I want you?"

My sugar walls started to melt as I clenched my legs together. The drink was making me forget all my inhibitions. I wanted to part his legs and climb in his lap.

"Yes Erick, I like you, too. I want you, too."

"Come closer Devan, why so far away?"

I got up and sat next to him, our knees touching. He slipped his hand into mine.

"You are so very beautiful, and that ass is fat too mama."

We shared a laugh. Then it got quiet again. I looked at him and inched my face closer to kiss the alcohol off of his lips. Oh my gosh, he was such a great kisser! My love cave became moist as I sucked his bottom lip. I thrusted my tongue into his mouth. He tasted so good! He cupped my face pulling me into him. Kissing me once more, he massaged my scalp. I moaned, slightly. I raised my body up as he rubbed my back and pulled my cami above my head. Then the unthinkable happened. His phone rang.

Chapter 10

Erick

I groaned inwardly as I snatched my phone out of my pocket. How embarrassing. It was that my pops was calling me as Devan and I shared a moment. I hurriedly answered and apologized for missing dinner with him and my mother. I told him I would be there tomorrow night. Powering the phone down, I looked sheepishly at Devan as she gave me a reassuring smile. I stared at her full pouty lips as she covered her breast with the cami she had taken off. I reached over and gently took the cami down to expose her caramel colored breasts and half dollar size nipples. I licked my lips sexily as Devan dipped her head. Tilting her head upwards, I kissed her lips sucking on her bottom lip, tasting the liquor residue as she moaned slightly.

"Do you want me to finish?" I asked her.

Moaning, she kissed me back giving me the green light to proceed. Devan got up to change the music on Pandora. She walked back to sit beside me. I gently grabbed her arm and stood her in front of me. I fondled her breast. First the left, and then the right breast as she rubbed my head in a circular motion. I pulled her leggings off to expose her purple, lace thong that gripped her hips and wide succulent ass. I was in awe that I was in this woman's presence and what we were about to do.

Pulling her thong off with my teeth, I came face to face with her hairless snatch and sniffed her womanly essence. She smelled of peach body wash, and I was going to love tasting her pearl. I trailed kisses from her neck to her stomach rubbing all over her body as she moaned and shivered.

Luther Vandross's "*If This World Were Mine*" serenaded us as I towered over her. Cupping her face, we shared a lengthy kiss. I was going to take my time with this body of hers. It was a canvas of art, and I was the painter. I laid her on the couch and stepped out of my clothes while I searched for the condom in my pocket. Devan looked on as I set the condom on the table and crawled between her legs. Taking her breast, I sucked, licked, and cupped her breast until her breathing became labored. She took her finger and began sucking on it as I gave her breast much needed attention.

Kissing her stomach, I moved down to the very spot I wanted to taste as Devan tried to stop me. I moved her hands away as I cupped her ass. I slid her down and opened her legs wide. I licked her clit nice and slow as Devan's leg shook. I smirked because that wasn't even the half of what I was about to do. Opening her pussy lips, I bent down, and tongue lashed her gently before picking up speed. She rotated her hips pulling me closer to her cave as I hummed to make vibrations against her clit. She squealed as I stuck my tongue in her vagina as if it was my dick.

I know I was giving it to her descent. She wrapped her legs around my shoulders as I turned her body towards the edge of the couch and continued to munch on her goodies. My dick was so hard, but I was determined to let her get her nut-or nuts before I released her. Her moans turned into screams, and I punished her kitty while I sucked, licked, and blew on her love box. I upped the ante as I slid my tongue over her asshole which caused her to buck and run from me. I slapped her ass and pulled her back. Diving back on her clit, it hardened. She was almost ready.

"Erick-KKK kk!" she screamed out as I licked faster and faster.

She started clawing at me. She pushed me back as I held onto her. Her legs shook violently, and her body was warm to the touch, but I wasn't letting go.

She grunted and shouted, "I'm cumming-GGG!"

Her sweet juices squirted out of her into my waiting mouth. I lapped it up as her body became rigid and fell back against the couch. I kissed her pearl, blowing on it as she gasped. That's when I went in for a second nut. I wasn't playing when I said I wanted to suck the soul out of her. My tongue lashing became too much for Devan as she bucked and screamed. I latched on, licking her sensitive clit. I inserted two fingers into her pussy as I continued to lick her up. I moaned in appreciation as I witnessed giving her so much pleasure.

"Are you ready to come again, babe?" I asked her as she shook and gyrated making those sexy ass sex noises.

"Argh, yes, yes, yes!" she screamed out as I zeroed in on her clit once more as it hardened in my mouth. She was on the verge of another orgasm, and I was the happy recipient. One more long flick of my tongue I gave her as she shook before warm, gushy juice filled my mouth as I slurped her dry. I winked as I looked up into her glazed eyes while she fought to catch her breath. I sat back proud of the work I had done so far. I waited for her to catch her breath. I had a whole lot more in store for this sexy ass woman.

Devan

Whew!! Oh my gosh, I was in a euphoric state. The things Erick did to my body would make a school girl blush! After his amazing tongue tricks, he carried me over his shoulders to my room. After laying me down on my bed, he grabbed my robe, took off the belt, and tied me to my bedpost. I was completely submissive as I let him have his way with me, and his girth! This man's tool was eleven inches in length and thick. For a moment, I was unsure whether I could handle his size, but he was gentle, yet thuggish as he worked his dick in my tight hole inch by inch.

I groaned and moaned as he gripped my ass to push inside of me deeper with confident strokes. I screamed his name as he bit my neck. He sucked and left deep purple passion marks. Erick then flipped me over and spread my ass cheeks wide and proceeded to taste my pearl from behind. Mmmm. As I rode his face, I gripped the bed sheets. He smack my ass.

He pushed my hand and in his gruff coarse voice ordered, "Tell me what you want me to do to you next Devan."

"Hmmm," I moaned. "Smack my ass."

SMACK!!! He smacked my ass and palmed it to make it jiggle.

"Again! Do it again!" I shouted.

I was on the verge of another orgasm. Erick obliged and smacked my ass over and over until I shouted and squirted my juices, coating his dick and the bed sheets. He abandoned my center to lap up my juices once again until there was no more.

I thought I was giving him all I had until he stroked his member to get another erection. I sexily licked my lips and took him into my mouth. Inch by inch, I sucked and made gurgling noises as his toes curled. I winked at him as he held my hair back and caressed my face. I knew I was giving him the business. His sex faces had me turned on, and I felt my pussy throb. Erick flipped me over, so I was on top of him. I was still amazed at how he could lift me up and toss me all over the bed. That alone made the inner freak come out of me. I was shying away from any awkwardness I ever felt about my weight because he can handle me. He rolled on another condom and reached up to sloppily kiss me.

"Get on this dick," he demanded while he stroked his shaft.

I smirked and moved down to insert his dick inside me. I moved slowly as I bounced up and down on his dick. stopping only to fuck the tip of his dick, I watched his face as he bit his lip in hopes of holding back his nut. He rubbed and sucked my breasts as I put my hands on his chest. I braced myself as I bucked back and forth as if I was a stallion, his stallion. Still, with his dick in me, I swiveled around with my back to his face as he grunted and muttered "Damn."

I rode him backward like a porn star as he smacked my ass over and over. Erick licked his finger and gently inserted it into my ass as I continued to ride his dick. We were both on the precipice of a mind-blowing orgasm. We fucked, we moaned, and we talked dirty to each other. No longer caring about my sexual inhibitions, I threw my head back and screamed as I gushed on his dick. He grabbed my hips pumping several times until he too came. He sat up with his arms wrapped around me as I felt him fill up the condom.

"Don't move!" He warned as I giggled at his sensitivity.

I moved slowly winding my hips, careful to take heed of his warnings. We both fell back on my bed as he spooned me, kissing me deeply and fingering my clit once more. As if I didn't think I could cum again, I did as he watched me with a satisfied grin. We laid in that position for a while before getting up to shower together. I was on cloud nine as I heard his light snores. Then, I turned over, and went to sleep as well.

Chapter 12

Erick

The weekend went by so fast. It was great! The amazing lovemaking Devan and I did was, by far, the best I have ever had. Besides the fact a few times my ex-girlfriend, Trish, kept calling and blowing up my phone, it was great. The next morning, I woke up to a home cooked breakfast. Man, that woman can cook! She had a spread of cheese grits, omelets, home fries, bacon, and sausage patties with coffee and orange juice. A meal fit for a king. Of course, I rewarded her with some more good dick.

I had her in the shower, on the couch, and even against the walls, all of them. I could tell Devan hadn't had a man pay this much attention to her body in quite some time. I mean I was hitting it right. I ate her kitty so much, that when I went to go near her, she scooted away from me because it was that tender. Of course, we didn't stay in bed all weekend. I took her around town in one of those carriages you can rent by the hour. We dined in some fancy restaurants, went to the opera, toured Detroit's most historical places, and topped it off with a stallion meal at a Hibachi Japanese place that has a waiting list months in advance.

The thing about Devan was that she was impressed with my connections and the places I showed her, but I could tell she was just a down home sweet girl, who didn't care about fame and notoriety. She just wanted to work, pay her bills, and just be with me. Of course, she went back to work. I had no qualms about that either. We kept it professional per her request, but everyone knew that she was mine.

Devan had a different aura about herself. Her walk was different. Well, I was hitting it every night and morning, when I stayed over at her condo. Sara was hella jealous of Devan, and I warned her about that. Sara wanted me to fuck her at one point, but I'm not into white women. Plus, Craig was doing the honors. However lately, Sara had been stopping by my office or asking for extra work she can do for me. Me being a man, I recognized her not so subtle advances and warned her about that. I had a feeling she was not going to take no for an answer.

Trish had been blowing up my phone, and I had a feeling she was going to get aggressive, especially since I wasn't answering her. I did, however, shoot her an email letting her know we were well past done, and I long since moved on from any and everything that existed with her. That email was sent three months ago. That was how long I and my love bug had been officially dating. Yes, Devan was finally mine, and I couldn't have been happier. Nothing could change that, or stand in the way.

Chapter 13
Erick

One Week Later.....

The day was like no other Tuesday morning. I had spent the night with Devan. We got off work, had dinner, and sexed the entire night. Now, we were having breakfast and on our way into work. We planned to go to Hershey, Pennsylvania for the weekend, and I was stoked. Getting off the elevator with Devan, I followed her to her desk setting her briefcase down in route to my office. She rewarded me with one of her dazzling dimpled smiles of hers as she sat down to begin her day. As I neared my office, Sara intercepted me with a few notes she had taken from the phones calls that came in while I was out. I thanked her, and she eyed me lustfully as I closed my door. Sitting down, I perused the notes from the clients until I came across one from Trish. Furrowing my brows, I scanned the note pinching the bridge of my nose. The note read;

Hey Doll! I know that you have been ignoring my calls, and you have every right to considering how I treated you. I want to apologize for my insensitiveness towards you. Erick, I still love you, and I am very much in love with you. Please, can you consider calling me back to rehash our issues and start over? My number is still the same. Trish.

To say I was annoyed was an understatement. What the hell could I possibly have to talk to her about? Trish left me! I tried to make it right. I tried to get us back on track with our relationship. She was the one who said she was bored with us, that sex with me was a chore, as opposed to being fun. She was the one who complained when I took on clients and worked 75 hour weeks. I tried, tried, and failed well, thought I failed.

Trish ended up walking out on me and us. That to me was unforgivable. Besides, I'm with Devan now, and she completes me. She understands me. She is aware of my long days and nights when a case demands our attention and sacrifice. She understands if I have to board a plane on an impromptu work-related thing suddenly. She gets me, we laugh, we share intimate moments, my parents like her, she can cook, and the sex, the sex was the bomb.

Trish did everything in the beginning to get me, and when she had me, she stopped trying. She couldn't cook, but I could, and I was fine with that. Trish spent my money and saved hers. I was ok with that. She shopped, hung out all hours of the night, had girl's nights out, and I was ok with that. That was until she brought that woman to my office and said she was leaving me for her. At first, I laughed and even thought of a threesome, but then I became furious because she played me for a fool. No, I didn't want that old baggage and drama. I was done with that. I have what I ever wanted in Devan.

Leaning back in my seat, I was lost in my thoughts. Looking out into the reception's room, the elevator chimed, and I heard a pair of heels click across the floor. Looking out my mouth dropped open as I saw a tall, slender woman approach Devan's desk and lean in to speak to her. At a time like this, I wished she would have just stayed away. That woman was Trish.

Chapter 14
Devan

AHHHHHHHHH! I was in bliss! I had my job back, well, I never lost it. Erick tore up my resignation letter the night he came to my house. It was awkward at first, but then he opened up and told me how he felt about me, prompting me to reveal myself to him as well. After that, we had the most awesome sex ever! I felt weird sleeping with him that night, and I told him so, but he told me I was ridiculous, especially since we were already feeling each other and our secret looks we gave each other as we passed each other in the office. After that, I gave zero fucks, let my hair down, and gave that man some of this good, gushy kitty. Now, three months later, we are dating, and it's been better than ever! This weekend we are going out of town to see some sights, dine, shop, and sex all over the suite he booked. Snapping back to reality, I grabbed the files to be completed for the day and began to work. Erick had sent an IM to my computer, and I blushed as I read it. He was so freaky, and I loved that about him. I planned to give it to him any way, place, or position that he wanted me in. He did mention his Ex often complained about the size of his dick, and I honestly feel sorry for her because he's all mine now and I can assure you that I can handle that big monster of his!

I had been working for a little over an hour, and I stopped to refill my cup of tea. Sitting back at my desk, I heard the elevator bell chime as I typed away at these files. I didn't notice the woman until she cleared her throat, causing me to look up. She was a pretty woman, tall and slender-or slim thick with a nice size ass and full 36c cups. She

ADD

adorned a black pants romper with red heels and a full side part illusion weave. Looking up, I smiled at her as she flipped her hair and spoke.

"Good morning, welcome to Jones, Jones, and Wallace, how may I help you?" I asked. She leered at me, picking imaginary lint off of her clothes.

"Devan, is it?" I nodded my head still smiling as she leaned forward. "Well bitch, you have something of mine, and I'm here to claim him back!" It took a few moments for me to get my bearings together as I stared at her blankly. It was at that moment. The past was staring at the future. I was looking into the eyes of Erick's ex-girlfriend Trish.

Chapter 15
Erick

Man, I really couldn't believe what I was seeing. Trish was standing by Devan all in her face. From the looks of it, Devan was holding her composure as Trish screamed at her with everyone looking on. I couldn't get out there fast enough. As I approached the ladies, Devan was speaking in a hushed tone.

"My apologies ma'am, but if you wish to speak to Mr.Jones, I will have to page him."

"Fuck all that!" Trish spat. "As I said before, you seem not to know your place as a secretary, so I'm here to help enlighten you. You are Not Erick's woman, I am, and I'm here to reclaim what's mine," she responded nastily. Devan's cheeks flushed bright red as she reared back to stand.

"As I have stated before, I"ll let Mr. Jones know you are here, but anything else that doesn't apply to this firm isn't your concern," Devan responded. I stepped in at that moment and gently, but firmly grabbed Trish and guided her towards my office.

"I"ll handle this, everyone back to work," I said. Devan looked at me with inquisitive eyes, and I shot her a look of apology. I definitely didn't mean for her to be in the middle of this bullshit. We were just starting out, and I planned to keep her around for a long while. "What the hell was that?" I growled at Trish once we were in my office.

"Erick, what the hell are you doing fucking the help?" she shot back.

"Devan is her name, and she is my woman, and she will not be disrespected, period," I said as she sneered at me.

"No! I'm sorry, but I cannot let that happen, Erick. W-We were meant to be. I mean yes I walked away from you, we had issues, I had to find my purpose, and what it was I wanted to do and what I wanted, but she needs to go, I'm here now, and there's no room for her," Trish said. I pinched the bridge of my nose letting out air from my mouth.

"Trish, you left me," "No," I said holding my hand out to stop her words. "I had a love for you at one point. You chose this. You walked away from us. Was I supposed to just wait for you like an ass?

"No, but you gave up too soon Erick, you didn't give us a chance or even closure for that matter."

"Trish, are you serious? Are you that blinded by your guilt, that you see no wrong in what you did? You left Me!" I shouted before lowering my voice. Several people looked in our direction toward the office door. "Look, Trish, I'm sorry, but it's over, and I cannot be with you, I care for you, but that's all. I've moved on, and it's best you do as well." She peered at me with tears falling from her pretty face.

"You don't mean that Erick," she whispered. "You simply can't just turn our love off that easy and walk away. It hasn't even been that long ago, I'm not accepting this."

"Look, Trish," I said sighing. "We have been over for quite some time now. I'm in a new relationship, and I hope someday you can accept that and be happy, but I'm sorry". Trish looked up and slapped me across my face.

"You bastard!" She hissed. "You let this bitch come in between us and fuck up our good thing, and you're telling me it's over! We will see about that! She turned around and stomped out of the office knocking over items on my desk. I sighed as I began picking the mess up. I have a feeling Trish will be back with more drama, and it was just the down-home.

Chapter 16
Devan

To say I was pissed was an understatement. This bitch waltzes in here calling herself regulating some shit when he doesn't want anything to do with her. I just hope she didn't think she had me shook. The only reason I didn't put on a show was that I need my job, and even though I was fucking the Boss, I was still a self-made woman, and I took care of myself. Yes, I was slightly embaressed when she walked by and called me a fat, dick riding whore as she got on the elevator. I literally had to let her have that comment because baby girl almost caught a major beat down! As on cue, Sara rolled her ass over to me from her desk, ready for some tea.

"Biiiiiiiiitch! what the hell?" she asked. Her eyebrows arched almost to her forehead.

"Well I guess she is coming back for her boo," I said using the quotation marks with my fingers.

"Psssssst, please!" Sara said. "Everyone knows Trish is very drama-fied, as long as I've been working here, she and Erick have been off and on."

"Yeah, well I'm not about drama. I just do my job and go home," I said clicking the tip of my pen repeatedly. I was still seething from the encounter.

"Yeah, and you also do Erick too!" Sara snorted. I shot her a look as I leaned closer.

"I do not want my personal life to correlate with my job Sara, so please lower your voice when you're talking," I said to her.

"Ok, ok, I gotchu," she agreed. "But, just so you know, Trish isn't a backdown kind of chick. She will be back with her shit. She's one of those bad and boujee bitches that shops and has the nice cars and shit like that. Be careful Devan," Sara warned.

"Yeah, sure, got it," I answered. I wasn't worried about that chick. Erick knew what it was. We were an item, and have been for a short while, a good, short while, but he and I were a thing and this bitch better come harder, because that man is all mine, and then some.

Chapter 17

Sara

Talking to Devan had me in stitches! Tyler and I were in the corner office literally sipping our tea watching tv! I had a feeling Devan was fucking Erick Jr. or at least was starting to fuck him. Hell, who didn't want that fine ass milk chocolate bar? I even tried to hit on him, but he was very professional at work, and not into white women. I was five feet three inches with strawberry blonde silky hair, that was shoulder length. I had features similar to the actress Angelina Jolie, with full pouty suckable lips, and round doe like green eyes. I had very tanned skin, thanks to my Italian family genetics. And my body? It was full of curves with an ass.

I was Mr. Craig Wallace's secretary for the firm Jones, Jones, and Wallace. Yes, I was also fucking him. I grew up near the 8-mile area in Detroit, around predominately black and Spanish people, and a sprinkle of whites as well. So, I dated mostly black guys in school, and I loved it.

Now, back to the drama at hand. I had to hide my smirk when Trish stormed up in here with her ghetto apologies bitch mantra, all up in Devan's face claiming she stole Erick and demanded him back. Ha! Man, the room was so freakin quiet waiting for her reaction. Hell, I thought Devan was going to react to match Trish's outlandish behavior. But, Devan kept her cool and maintained her pretty girl cool. I bet that Devan wanted to tear Trish's face apart! I got my Mac lipstick and applying more gloss to my lips. I dug in my purse to send my boo a text message. No, not Craig. He was my sugar daddy who fucked me good, paid off my college debts, and laced my account monthly. As for payment in return, I fucked and sucked him decent. He couldn't get enough of my sweet peach. I gave it to him on his desk, chair, and even his car at times when I took a lunch break. He wasn't my ideal guy, hell, he wasn't that good looking, but he was paid.

Looking over my shoulder, as I texted Quan back, Tyler sucked in his breath.

"Ooh bitch, Quan ass is so fine," he cooed.

"Yes, he is," I agreed. "And he's mine, so back off honey."

"Oh girl, whatever, just continue to keep him happy, or I'd have to take him from you!" He joked.

"Ha ha, yeah ok, Quan has all he needs right here," I said as I ran my hands up and down my body as we laughed.

I looked over at Devan as she worked. She was my girl and all, we weren't besties, but she was cool. I decided to up the ante and have a little fun with her and secretly flirt with Erick. Hell, maybe he might give in and give me some of that chocolate. He had a lot on his plate as it is with Trish resurfacing. I chuckled as I conjured up ways to be devilish.

Chapter Eighteen
Erick

I leaned back in my chair, plowing in my mind over the events that just took place. Who the hell did Trish think she was? I mean, we tried to make it work, or at least I did, but she's just a money hungry, selfish woman who was very materialistic. I craved more mental, physical, and emotional trust. Things that I know Trish couldn't and wouldn't provide. There was no way I was ever going back to that! Peering out into the main office, I looked at Devan hard at work. Snatching the phone off the charger, I dialed her line. I grabbed my stress ball and began squeezing as I listened to the number of rings before she picked up.

"Jones, Jones, and Wallace, Devan speaking, how may I direct your call?" she asked, as her soft melodious voice sang out into the receiver.

It made my tool stiffen at her voice as I imagined kissing her soft gloss covered lips.

Clearing my throat, I answered her. "Yes, ah please come into my office for a moment."

"Right away," she responded disconnecting our call.

A moment later soft taps could be heard on the door as I called out, "come in." My love came in the door in a sexy one-piece black pants romper with a shawl covering her arms. Her hair was braided up in a 'high bun.' She was the most beautiful woman I'd seen, and she was all mine. Getting up, I crossed the room. I closed the blinds and locked the door. I turned around to face her, planting soft kisses on her mouth. She pushed me back slightly as she nervously looked towards the door.

"We're at work Erick," she said.

" I know," I replied, as I wrapped my arms around her.

Bringing her closer to me, I kissed her again. At first, she was stiff but loosened up as a soft moan escaped her mouth. I broke the kiss and stared deep into her eyes.

"I want to apologize to you for earlier. I had no idea she was even in town, let alone coming to my job in the way she did. She did send me an email wanting to talk to me, but I wasn't in any mood to entertain her. I'm sorry babe. It won't happen again."

"Oh yes, it will happen again," Devan insisted. "That woman shared a relationship with you and didn't get any closure. So, she will come back unless you talk to her and get some clarity."

"Devan," I started, "I have no qualms about even speaking to her at this point. I simply wish her the best in her life and her endeavors. That's it. I will, however, invite her to lunch, and I will hear what she has to say, but I've moved on, with you, and I wish not to dwell on the matter any longer."

I could see a hint of doubt flash in her eyes, and it was gone just that quickly. I needed Devan to know that I was hers and she was mine. She was the only woman for me. All of her.

Chapter 19
Devan

God, I was feeling this man. The way his aura screams 'take charge,' I felt comfortable in his arms. Here I was thinking she was coming in here to get some straightening and take him back. I thought I was going to be left out on my ass with no man, and no job. However, what Erick and I shared was deeper than that in such a short amount of time. I was confident enough to know my spot was secured with him. Looking up into his eyes, I saw love, lust, and respect and I was feeling fulfilled and content. He for sure was getting some tonight.

"So, I guess that was enough excitement for one day eh?" I asked him as he spooned with me as we stood erect.

He was too busy grabbing my ass while palming it and licking his lips as if he wanted to fuck me here in his office. Hmmm, just like my fantasy I had awhile back. Licking his lips as he toward over me, he dipped his head to suck on my lips as I kissed him back fervently. He cupped my breasts pinching my nipples as my head went back. Erick unclasped my top pulling my romper down my back to my feet as I stood clad in my bustier and panty set. I was nervous for someone to knock on the door, or worse call him while we were in the middle of whatever he was about to do to me.

Erick reached down and picked up my clothing setting it on a chair, as he knelt down face to face with my love box. He smelled my peach as he nibbled on my clit through my panties. A low gasp escaped my lips as I rubbed his head guiding him closer to her. He slid my panties down to my feet, and I stepped out of my them. Clearing a space on his desk, he guided me to sit on top of it. I obliged as I happily waited for what was next. Erick walked toward me licking his lips as he smirked at me.

"I'm about to taste my pussy," he said gruffly.

My clit throbbed as I became wetter and I leaned back and opened my legs welcoming him to my center. He pulled up a chair and sat directly in front of me as he opened my legs wider and dove in. My legs shook as I laid back to receive his tongue lashing. The threat of being caught in his office mixed with our low moans and the vibration of his tongue was sending my mind into overload as I face fucked him back. His tongue swirled around my clit slowly as he stuck his finger in my pussy, twirling it around gathering my love juice out of me as he slurped. He bit down on my clit adding some pain before he kissed and sucked welcoming pleasure. I stuck my finger in my mouth to suck on it, so I wouldn't scream out loud, almost forgetting where we were.

"Look at me while I'm eating you out Devan," Erick commanded as I got even wetter at his request.

"Ssssss y-yes, right there, faster, yea, ooh ooh sss!" I rambled on.

He was taking me on a fantastic voyage as he dipped his tongue in and out of me as if it was a dick. His sex game was definitely 100%. Erick reached around palming my ass spreading it wider as he continued to feast. I knew I was on a precipice of an orgasm and he was not stopping. He finger fucked me as I got wetter drowning his beard. He moaned and slurped as he stuck his finger in my asshole and another in my pussy. In and out he went, simultaneously picking up speed licking my clit. I felt my clit harden as my legs shook. A warm sensation came over me as I pinched my nipples and licked them.

"Ooooh Erick, I'm cumming!" I moaned as I bucked and my cum squirted out into his waiting mouth. He loudly slurped me until I was dry and I fell back on the desk in a daze. He sat up and smirked that sexy ass smile at me as I used my finger motioning for him to kiss me tasting myself on his lips.

"There's definitely more waiting for you at home tonight," he whispered in my ear making me shiver slightly. Erick got up and came back with a warm washcloth and cleaned me up as I got up to get dressed. We wiped down the desk and straightened up before I kissed him and went to the conference room in the back to walk around front away from curious eyes and ears. If I had any doubt from earlier, it was most certainly wiped out after our encounter. I just hoped I was more than woman enough to keep and hold his attention on me. I made it to my desk to grab my purse to go with Sara to lunch.

Chapter 20

Sara

I decided to meet at Applebee's for lunch with Devan and Tyler. I wanted to pick her brain about her lover and find out why she was in his office for so long. Was one of us getting fired? Were we getting a new intern? Tuh! She was in there fucking his brains loose. I thought to myself as I looked over the lunch menu. I ordered a watermelon Sangria and water with lemon as I watched Devan walk in the door towards me. I got the waitress' attention again as Devan neared.

"Um yes, my lunch date is here so she will be ordering her drink," I explained to the waitress.

"Yes, ok hello, and what can I get you, ma'am?" she asked Devan as she got out her pen and pad.

"Ahh, please let me have a glass of white wine and also a water with lemon." The waitress nodded her head and once completing her order, turned, and walked to bring the order. I sized Devan up as she sat down and looked around the busy restaurant. It seemed like everyone chose here to come to lunch today.

"So, I started off, what happened back there in Mr. J's office? Did you get paddled for your outburst with Trish?" I amusingly taunted her.

Devan stared blankly at me and told me to shut up before I snorted at her and laughed as Tyler side eyed her and turned up his lip.

"Aww, come on D," I said, "no really, what happened?"

Devan cocked her head to one side and responded.

"Nothing happened if you must know."

"I must," I retorted, "you were back there an awfully long time," I stuck my straw in my water and slurped as I watched the waitress bring Devan her drink order.

She looked relieved as she tore the paper off her straw and drank down her sangria, signaling the waitress to bring one more. Tyler nursed his peach margarita as he scrolled his Instagram, hearing hustling to us.

I guess it was happy hour because none of us ordered food yet. I side eyed Devan as she checked her phone and happily took her second drink from the waitress. What the hell did Erick see in her? To me, she seemed too put together and not all that freaky in the bedroom. He needed a woman like me to put it down on him. Hell, I'd give it to him anytime. Anal beads, plugs, torture chamber, sex chair, nipple rings, in the rain, the subway like Tom Cruise in 'Risky Business,'.

Hell, I'd be his sexy white slave. He could choke me until I damn near pass out as he nutted. My panties creamed at that last thought, as I fantasized over Erick. I know when I get back to the office, I was jumping on Craig's dick. Hell, I had to get my rocks off with him, until I cou;d seduce Erick. We will see if miss priss can hold a candle to me.

We made small talk as we had our lunch cocktails. We both ordered a Mediterranean chicken salad to go. I surmised Devan wasn't going to talk about her office tryst with me or anyone. Devan pulled off a few bills for her tab, stood, and said her goodbyes, leaving Tyler and me there to talk about her ass. I mean we weren't besties or anything. We would all go out to the club or dinner and such, but friends, definitely not.

"Girl, now you know she was slobbing on that chocolate bar," Tyler said making a motion with his fist toward his mouth.

I laughed and co-signed as we slapped a high five. I had plans of my own with said chocolate bar as well, I sneakily masterminded. We finished our drinks, paid our tab, and left with our to go box. I was ready to put my plan into action. I think I'll call it Operation big dick. I laughed as if something Tyler had said was funny as we exited the restaurant to go back to work.

Chapter 21

Sara

Upon returning to the office, I quickly dropped my belongings at my desk and grabbed my coffee mug as if I was going to the breakroom. I made a detour to the left, passed the breakroom, and continued down the hall further as Craig's office suite was a bit further down than Erick's. I barged in his room as I always do, without knocking. He swiveled around in his chair, gleaming at me lustfully. I wasted no time locking the door and dropping to my knees to crawl in between him.

He is so freaky, I thought.

Craig was leaned back in his chair, deep in a business conference with his pants already unzipped and shirt disheveled. He must have been jerking off way before I even thought to come back this way, I gathered. I pulled his pants down further as he lifted up to allow me access. For a man his age, he was working with a big tool, and although he wasn't as fine and ripped as Erick was, he definitely fucked me good and kept my bank account fed.

I never hesitated to please him whenever and however. Which was why I was here, groping his meat and jerking him to another erection as my mouth salivated. Yeah, I was a freaky bitch who loved big dick. I started talking to Mr. Big Dick cooing and purring on the shaft as I stroked slowly up and down, up and down. Craig loved when I did this. Who said there wasn't any more power in the pussy? Tuh!! I licked his shaft as I stared into his eyes. He watched me suck him off. My clit was getting moist as I slipped out of my black pencil skirt, preparing to take all of his girth. Craig finished his phone call and directed his attention to me. He grabbed the T.V. remote control, and turned up the volume on *Sports Center.* Yeah, he was a moaner, and I happily brought that out of him.

"AHHH, you're such a little nasty bitch, eh?" Craig cooed.

"Mmmph, slurp, lick, gurgle," was my response.

Craig threw his head back as I cupped his balls and stretched my mouth to allow his dick to slide down my throat reaching my tonsils easily. I moaned and groaned as I continued to please my 'money sponsor,' as for sure after this fuck fest he was going to deposit an extra $5,000 into my account. As a precaution, I have a locked code that I used so he or no one else couldn't go back and retract any monies that I had accumulated. Yeah, I was a smart bitch and didn't play about my coins!!

After I got his 'full attention,' standing up high with a slight right hook. I stood up to admire my handiwork. There little man was, all glistening and shining, wet from my spit and waiting for miss kitty to talk to him.

"Come here to daddy," Craig said as he reached his hand to grab mine. I swatted his hands away as I strip teased him. I unbuttoned my top slowly, as I bit my bottom lip suggestively, further teasing him. Craig started grunting and loosening his tie, as he broke out into sweat.

"I'm gonna make you feel really good, just sit back and relax daddy," I said as I stood before him stark naked.

I strolled over to him as he licked his lips. He pulled me into him as my breasts hit him in his face. He wasted no time cupping my left breast, licking and sucking as he fondled my right. I sucked in a breath and moaned in pleasure, getting my breast sucked was a euphoric feeling. I let Craig take a little control before I mounted him to give him the ride he was looking for.

He looked up at me as he continued licking me as his finger slide into my folds and finger fucked me. A sigh escaped my lips once more as his large fingers worked me over. Craig stood up and laid me on the couch adjacent to his desk as I got comfortable to receive some much-needed tongue lashing. After relieving himself of his shirt and tie, Craig was on his knees, pushing my legs up to my chest as he dove in and licked and sucked on my clit. I moaned and grabbed my breasts twisting my nipples as he snacked on my gushy center. He could really eat some pussy! That's why I kept my legs near his face as often as possible. I let out a giggle as I thought how shady Tyler was going to be as I recounted my 'smash session' with Craig.

Craig thought my outburst was about him as he stopped abruptly to look at me curiously. I quickly pushed his head back down to finish his deed as I felt my body getting warm to unleash a much deserved 'O.' At last! I felt my body tense up as Craig slid his finger in my ass and he continued to feast.

"FUCK!!" I creamed all over Craig's mouth as he greedily lapped up my juices. I was spent, but he wasn't.

"Give me a moment," I told him out of breath, as I watched him sit on the couch stroking himself to another erection.

He reached into his pockets and slid on a condom as I begrudgingly sat up to slide down his shaft. My only incentive was that I imagined it being Erick's dick, and that gave me a boost of energy. I wasn't a big fan of kissing, and Craig knew that, and he always tried to slide his tongue in my mouth, but this time I surprised him as I bit his lower lip and sucked and kissed him passionately. Just like he did my pussy moments before.

I put my hands on his shoulders and got into a squatting position as he placed his hands under my thighs to help me balance. I closed my eyes, and I imagined fucking Erick to Joe's hit song, '*More and More.*' I bounced, I swirled, I rotated my hips, I rocked, and I even did a splitting position on that dick. I laughed inwardly at Craig as he thought this was for him. I even pulled out some new tricks even he hadn't been privy to! His dick got rock hard. I knew his time had come. He tried to hold off as long as possible, but I knew his weakness as I twisted his nipples hard.

He grunted, yelped, and then licked them with my warm, wet mouth. A little bit of pain and pleasure was Craig's guise. He spread my ass cheeks wider and gave me three hard thrusts and burst his seed into the condom as I reached down and fingered my clit bringing my orgasm to the surface. Spent, Craig threw his head back catching his breath as I nibbled on his chin and stroked his ear.

Yeah, I earned my money and then some! I needed a new outfit to go out this weekend, and for Monday... something new that Erick hasn't seen yet. Hopping off Crag's lap, I gathered my clothes to shower in his private bathroom. After washing up, I grabbed a washcloth, wet it with soap and came out to a suspecting Craig, still in the same position. I cleaned him up and even helped pull his pants back up. I put on an Award-winning performance, and I knew it.

After brushing my teeth and fixing my hair, I made myself a cup of his hazelnut coffee with the mug I left my station with. I crossed the room and sat on the edge of the desk as Craig pulled up his bank account info and transferred money into my account. $5,000 as the norm. Then he went into his safe and handed me an extra $2,000. I was elated. I bent down and kissed him. I told him I would be back tomorrow for an encore. I groped his dick making it jump. I patted his shoulders and retreated to my seat. Tyler looked over at me, and I gave him a sheepish grin. He clucked his tongue at me and mouthed the words 'cunt' as I continued my work tasks, anxious to leave for some retail therapy.

Chapter 22
Erick

Two weeks later.

Work was work. I had dove into mass trials and hearings that kept me pretty busy most nights. Luckily for me, I had a spare room converted into a bedroom when I didn't want to go all the way home. Devan would come by, bring me dinner she cooked, or we would go to a steakhouse to eat and talk. My feelings for her were growing rapidly as if they would change? Nope. Amid all of the phone call, texts, and emails Trish sent, all went unanswered. I didn't want to risk upsetting Devan and making her feel that Trish had a chance. Yeah, at some point a conversation will have to happen, but now I was good on that; but not knowing Trish was going to make that happen herself, and soon.

I called Devan up to see when she was coming over. I needed to feel her warm body, and I wanted to taste some of the her-my delicious peach between her legs.

"Hello?" Devan answered the phone.

"Hey bae, it's me."

"Hey me, she giggled. "How was your day?"

" Aww man, rough, I started out. But waiting on your sexy ass to come sit on daddy's dick," we shared a laugh, and she told me was coming soon and she missed me as well. Although we see each other daily, lately she was on another floor helping Dorinda with renovations, and the other half of the day in the office; so we snuck in time for lunch, a kiss, or a quickie in my office.

"Ok babe, I'll see you then, and oh hey, wear that v-neck dress I got for you. You know the one that barely covers you? You won't be wearing it for long anyhow." I solidified.

"Ha ha! Ok, bae, I gotcha, see you soon," she said.

I stood up and stretched the day's stress away and walked over to the mini bar pouring me a shot of Hennessey. Pouring another shot, I sat back in my chair and closed my eyes. Listening to the cleaning crew in the main room tidying up after a full day of work. I realized I had dozed off in a mini nap when I heard a knock on my door as Roberto, the head janitor, opened the door.

"Mr. Jones, I'm sorry to interrupt, but there's a woman here for you, she says you are expecting her?" he queried.

"Ahh, ok, yes, please send her in, thanks."

I reached in my drawer for some gum as I heard the clicking of heels. I smirked because there wasn't going to be any eating, well, not dinner anyhow. As I looked up, I froze when my face rested on her. I stared blankly as she walked in smiling.

"Oh, don't be sad to see me, hun," Trish smirked.

"What the fuck are you doing here and who let you in? Roberto!" I yelled as I stood up and brushed past Trish. Roberto came running back toward me, face flushed, as I stopped in front of him.

"Why the fuck would you let her in here?"

"I'm so sorry boss," he rushed out. "Sh-she told me you were expecting her and it was ok!"

"That's fine, don't worry about it, you can go now," I released him for the evening, as I pinched the bridge of my nose in anger. I let out a deep sigh as I turned on my heels and trudged back into my office where Trish was reclining rather comfortably on my couch as if zero fucks were given.

"Alright, make this shit short and simple so that you can leave," I said as I sat back down and glared at her.

Trish flicked imaginary dirt off her dress as she blew out air from her lips.

"Damn Erick, we aren't strangers ya know. What's with the attitude?"

"Get to the point Trish, NOW!!"

"Fine, Erick, I love you, still do, I want you to come back home to me, to what we had. I'm sorry," she said as she looked to the floor.

I bit the inside of my cheek before answering.

"As you may know already, Devan is my woman, and I plan on her being my woman for now and in the future. You made that fatal decision bringing another woman into my relationship and not only lying to me but disrespecting me. You had a problem with me, you discussed our issues, sex life, you told me I was too big for you, and you couldn't handle me, or was it a ploy to pick reasons to argue and leave? Which is it? Huh?" I was mad, but to move on, I told Devan I would allow her to get her closure. To finally close that chapter of my past, and move the fuck on.

Trish huffed, "Erick, I'm sorry, I was wrong, and I admit it now, I do. I had issues, deep-rooted issues, and she, she came in at a time when I needed a distraction. I was wrong for cheating and being deceitful. You were, you are a good man, and you didn't deserve that. I just wish you would've given me a decent chance, us a chance before you got with her. She's a secretary, your secretary?" Trish snickered.

"Ok, that's enough, now what you will not do is talk about my woman that way," I barked at her. She stiffened in her seat. "I'm just here to help you get closure, and that's it, anything after that is a wrap, on us our friendship, and our relationship. You barge in here unwelcomed, texts, calls and emails, it has to stop! Please! I've heard you, listened, and I'm not swayed, so therefore if you're done, see yourself out." I exhaled after saying what I needed her to hear. She was not going to mess up what devan, and I created, for damn sure!

Trish started to sniffle as she wrung her hands. She knew my weakness, and I hated to see women cry. Although my facial expression was stoic, my eyes softened a tad bit, but I was NOT backing down.

"Trish, I don't mean to make you cry, but I put up with a lot from you these last six months while maintaining my job. You were out there with her without a care in the world, not even caring if we were on page five of *The Detroit Times* with your messiness. I mean hell, you tried to exploit me and drag my name through the mud. All the while, I stayed true to myself, gave you money, financed trips that I found out you took with her, might I add, and now you come up here on some get back with me crap? Oh no, no, Hell no Ma, I'm sorry, I'm good, but I do wish you the best in life, I really do." I said a mouthful.

However, you know the feeling when you did all you could, but you feel that person could be, or was almost retarded? Yep, I felt that as Trish wiped her tears, stood up, and crossed the room and stood in front of me.

"You don't mean that Erick, you don't. We shared six years today. We have history. Please don't do this," she said as she hiked up her dress. "Shh, just let me make it right, just please don't say no," she said as she lowered her mouth towards mine. Maybe it was the alcohol, but for a brief moment she had my dick rising, but I quickly snapped out of it and gently pushed her away as she grabbed my dick through my pants and he jumped. I won't lie, her touch felt good, and little man was trying to deceive and bend her ass over this desk, but her ass isn't what I wanted, I wanted my Devan.

"No, NO!" I yelled out, as I backed up in my chair. "You have to go, Trish, I'm sorry."

"No," she said as she grabbed my dick, attempting to unzip and free him," just let me put it in and sit on it. Please, I want this, you want this, PLEASE!"

At this point I jumped up and grabbed both her arms and held them to her side, being careful not to rub up against her. I was through with her, and I meant it, but she wasn't any the wiser. I loved and cared for Devan, and having a scandal in the office was not something I wanted or needed.

"I will let you go once you are calm, but do not try anything, you have to go, and now, I mean it," I forcefully instructed her as she sobbed trying to lean into me. It was hella awkward, kind of like giving your sister in Christ a church hug, without your genitals touching. Man!

"Erick no! Please, I need you, please!" she begged as she sobbed harder.

"I believe he asked you to leave now, as in now!" came a voice from behind me. Immediately my body tensed as I looked over at Devan, not knowing when she got there, or even how long she was standing there. Even though I didn't do anything, I felt guilty as hell, damn! WTF am I going to do now? I looked from Trish to Devan as

Trish smirked devilishly while Devan wore a pissed off scowl on her face.

Here we go!

Chapter 23
Devan

Imagine my surprise, upon arriving late to the firm bringing Erick and my dinner with wine, to find this, this trollop of a woman clinging on to him so desperately. Granted, men can be suspect of infidelity as well, but his saving grace was that I heard most of the conversation between the two as Trish was screaming like a banshee and begging for him to take her back! Ha! Man, please. After she humiliated him so terribly and openly and then showed her fucking dick sucking face at the firm and got in my face about my man!? What the hell?? So, here I am putting a stop to all of this nonsense once and for all and reclaiming what is mine. Leaning on my right leg hand on hip, I stood frowning at her while Erick kept looking from me to her. He looked as if he was caught with his proverbial hand in the cookie jar if you will; while this cunt sneakily cast her eyes towards me.

"Because I know what I know creating this drama filled cry for help 'woe is me' bullshit, which by the way, is pathetic as hell, I'm asking you again to leave."

"Bitch, and do what?" Trish snorted. "I was having a private conversation with him, one that didn't require a third party, so if you don't mind."

"Oh, yes, I do mind," I retorted. "He and I are having dinner; for whatever reason you came, you got what you wanted, or didn't want, he told you what was up, so now you leave." I was running out of patience with her, and it was like talking to a child.

Erick cleared his throat and co-signed; " Trish you have to go, thank you for coming by, but I said all that is to be said."

Trish looked from me to Erick and opened up a slew of curse words.

"You two fucking idiots are hilarious! You would rather fuck this fat beastly ass bitch than have all of this thickness?" She said as she ran her hands up and down her body. "I mean come the fuck on Erick! I said we could work this out, but you act like our six years and your six months are even worth not fighting for! What the fuck does she possess that I don't have? Huh?"

"Loyalty," Erick stated. It's simple. Man, Trish's face went from buttercream flavored to crimson red. She looked at Erick for what seemed five long minutes and turned knocking the lamp off the table towards him as he ducked while I stepped aside. Storming past me, she flicked her hair and stopped directly in front of me; I prepared myself for a fight if needed.

She leaned in and snarled, "You will never replace me bitch, while he's fucking you his mind will always be on me," she huffed and hightailed it towards the elevators as I looked on.

As I turned and looked at Erick, he started to apologize. "Bae, I'm sorry she was even here, I didn't know it was her unti-"

I stopped him as I held my hand up. "It's ok Erick, better now then never, or worse in a much more open place with lots of witnesses, eh?" He looked at me almost defeated as he helped me with the bags he had just noticed I was holding. I brushed the shit off my shoulders as I laid the food out after reheating its contents, poured the wine, said our grace, and sat down to eat. Was I sure the drama with her was over? Ah, hell no, but I was mature and woman enough to dismiss her ass and let my man handle his business. If it became physical, then I'd have to beat her ass.

One week later...

Some time had passed, and neither Erick nor I heard anything from Trish. I was always taught there was the calm before the storm, and that was what was to become that fateful Thursday. Some calls and emails were incoming on both of our phones and computers. I would get at least ten calls a day with hard, labored breathing, or high pitch screeching. I had to pull the phone away from my ear it was loud. I surmised it was Trish all the while, and dare I ask why I kept answering the phone? Simple, some clients would call from jail, and we had to keep our calls unblocked to allow access to them; our clientele went as far as the jail or prison, which is why I would answer the phone. Yes, keeping my professional hat on the whole time; when I wanted to offer her a slew of curse words to make her think about her actions as a child. I had to digress and entertain this poor excuse of a female. Five o'clock rolled around, and it was busy as it could ever be when Trish came strolling off the elevator in her element, head held so high you could see into her nostrils. Her usual weave was laid right, and she strutted in her Jimmy Choo's over to my desk and slung her bag down. I finished typing up a transcript oblivious to her rant, and as I fished, I looked up at her and gave a small, yet irritated smile.

"What can I help you with today?" I inquired uninterested.

"First of all bitch, you can cut the act and get Erick out here now!" she sneered.

I thought to myself that If she was that bad bitch, she could've simply gone into his office and got him herself. As if reading my mind,

Trish looked up into Erick's office and was about to head over when he walked out. His face was twisted into a scowl as he crossed the room rolling up his sleeves of his shirt.

"What the hell are you doing here now Trish?" he growled.

Trish pointed a manicured nail at his face.

"We are not done, you and her? Done, finished, what more do I have to do to convince you of that?" she retorted.

"As if it weren't enough that you hacked our computers and phones, stalking me at my house and place of business, what else is there Trish? Huh? No, don't even answer, the police are on their way. This is just too much, and I'm tired of it." Erick shouted back.

"You are sick? You?" Trish threw her head back and cackled. Mr. Wallace and Mr. Jones Sr. had run up to the front through the commotion. Both tried to talk Trish from over the edge. She had a crazed look in her eyes as she spun around and knocked my computer and whatnots off the desk. I stood up and moved aside now in a pissed off state of mind. My menstrual cycle was on and ladies you all know what that meant. I was bloated, irritated, cramping, tired and now, worked up. So, if this bitch wanted this stress I had on me, she was going to get it today. Trish kicked off her shoes and ran around the room yelling and cursing throwing flowers on the carpet and kicking over trash cans. She knocked over the copy machine and grabbed a stapler and chucked it in my direction. I ducked, and it hit my shoulder.

"Oh, hell no!" I shouted as I kicked off my heels and charged her. Erick tried to grab me as I shook him and dodged as the football players do. My hands reached Trish before I did. I grabbed her long weave, wrapped it around my hand and began pummeling her ass.

"Arggghhh! Oww get this bitch off of me!" she screamed. She was no match for these hands. Tyler and Sara jumped up to help Erick grab me and pry my hands off of her. No one heard the police come and as they shouted over us.

"Alright listen, break it up!" an officer shouted. I came back to my senses huffing and puffing as I picked Trish's weave off my hands.

"Officer, arrest her, she attacked me!" Trish screamed as a female office grabbed Trish's hands to detain her.

"Quiet down!" the first officer yelled as Trish writhed and screamed as the lady officer held her. Erick spoke up as he left my side to speak to the officer.

"Sir, please excuse the circus she has created, this is clearly an office work environment. This is my ex, the woman whom I made the report about the computer hacking into my personnel files." He explained.

Officer Maguire nodded his head. "Thank you, sir. We can handle it from here."

He turned to Trish as he began Mirandizing her. "Ma'am, you have a right to remain silent, anything you say or do-

"WHAT THE FUCK ARE YOU DOING? She is the one who attacked ME!" Trish screeched as the officer finished the Miranda rights. Trish twisted and kicked as both officers slammed her over my desk to handcuff her. She let out a horrendous guttural animal sound as if she were being slaughtered. Everyone watched in horror as she was escorted into the elevators. Erick straightened up his shirt and looked around the room.

"Alright everyone, that's enough excitement for today, Sara, please call Roberto to get his team to come and clean up. Everyone go home for today, be back bright and early tomorrow. I apologize for the inconvenience." The buzzing began as everyone gathered their belongings to leave, no one cared about leaving early, that was a treat for them. Erick looked at me as he came over and rubbed my arms up and down.

"Are you ok baby? I'm so, so sorry about that."

"Nah, I'm good," I replied as I began picking up around my desk. I was ready to go home and soak in the tub. My body was going to be sore in the morning.

"Damn, you kicked her ass like Mayweather did McGregor! Let me find out if you got some boxing skills!" he joked.

"Haha," I said as I tossed my cup at him. He caught it as he laughed. After I finished cleaning up, I gathered my things to leave. I waved goodbye to Erick and promised to wait up when he was ready to come by, with dinner of course. Today was a long day.

Chapter 24

Erick

Man, what a night. Hell, what a few, last few weeks. Between being bogged down with paperwork and clients, my ex- crazy ex-girlfriend blows back in town on some get back shit which I was not down for. That entire scene was like a page out of the Bad Girl's Club. Well, Trish didn't get was she was looking for but got what she didn't want, which was a shit load of jail time. I don't quite know how much jail for hacking, but she was going to be in jail for some time. Looking over at my baby Devan, I was very pleased and proud at how she carried herself with that confrontation. She caught me looking at her and shyly averted her eyes, and I gently grabbed her chin turning her back to face me. I leaned down toward her and gave those suckable pink lips of hers a peck, and then went in for a sensual kiss. She parted her mouth and allowed me full access as I trailed my tongue over her top and bottom lips tasting her peach flavored lip gloss. Shorty was fine as hell to me, and no matter what Trish said or how she tried to berate her about her weight, at the end of the day, I was giving her all of this dick, and then some.

Devan was past the fucking at the office at random times of the day by now. At first, she was nervous about getting caught, and or if people would hear and talk, but as quiet as we kept, we mostly fooled around in the rear of my office next to the debriefing room. Hell, Craig did his dirt, and I do mean dirt in his office, as well as other offices after hours with many of the secretaries from different floors. I wonder if Sara knew that, and I also wonder If she knew Craig was on the DL- Down low and has messed around with Tyler's crazy white ass! Hmm, that remains to be found out. I did, however, notice lately that she has reverted to the past and has been openly flirting with me again.

Before, when I was with Trish, she had to step to Sara a few times to nip that shit in the bud. Sara stopped, of course, but that didn't stop her from wearing low-cut blouses, thigh-high skirts, and nude color dresses, or the fact that she would bring my mail when that wasn't necessarily her job, but going out of her way to do so. I paid it no mind, but I figure I'd have to talk to her again now that everyone clearly knows who and what Devan is to me. I know they often went out for lunch or cocktails, work events, but I'm feeling Devan isn't all that keen on her. I just hope I'm done with any more potential drama/scandal and just focus on my baby. She's more than enough woman for me.

I draped my arm around her as we sat back to watch 'Baywatch' starring Zac Effron and Dwayne 'Rock' Johnson. Devan picked the movie. Hell, we both needed a laugh after that debacle. After the movie, I grabbed our trash tossing it as Devan wiped down the tables. I shut the light off and grabbed her shoes and purse after locking my part of the office up. I grabbed her hand and escorted her to the side door of my office that led to a spare bedroom. I transformed it for when I needed to stay and work late after hours.

Devan also had some clothes here when she would stay, and on those days, she got up, showered, dressed, and left for the cafe downstairs. Then, she came back up at the appropriate work hour when everyone filed in their respective destinations. She preferred it that way, to keep drama and naysayers at bay. It didn't bother me at all, but what my baby wanted, my baby got.

Joining her in the shower after I stripped out of my clothes, I welcomed the hot, steamy water as soon as it hit my body. I stood in the back of Devan admiring her thick, curvaceous frame as she lathered her body in Tangerine scented body wash from *Bath and Bodyworks*. I grabbed the body wash, poured some into my hands, and began washing and massaging her body as she let out a small moan. She leaned her body onto mine as I wrapped my arms around her fondling her breasts with soap. She reached back and grabbed my dick stroking him to an erection. He was rock hard.

After a trying day, I was ready to stick him into something warm and wet. Bending her over, I inserted myself into her warm slit and held myself there reveling in her delicious folds. Damn it was always like the first time when I slid in Devan. Her pussy was always wet and ready for me. Her pussy was responding to my dick like a hand to a baseball glove; we just fit each other. Devan threw her leg over the railing as I started rocking in and out of her water cave. Gushy sounds squirted on my dick each time I went in and out. I pulled out of her and left only the tip of my shaft as she moaned twirling her body. It drove her crazy. I reached around and squeezed her clit rubbing her pearl as I continued pushing in her guts. Dropping to my knees after pulling out, I opened her ass cheeks to her treasure and ate her from behind as she screamed my name. I slurped, she yelped, I shook my head from side to side vibrating on her pussy. She moaned and rode my face just how I like it. I inserted my finger in her pussy fingering her as she did her best to hold on. Her clit got hard; she was ready to cum. She pumped on my face concentrating on her orgasm, but I was aware of what she was doing.

"Oh, hell naw, I'm not ready for you to come yet," I said as she whimpered.

I wanted her to cum fast and hard. I stood back up and Inserted my dick into her once more as she looked behind her and bit down on her lip making me harder; she was teasing me, I had a trick for that I mused. Picking up speed, she fell in line and matched my strokes. We went on like this for a few minutes. She was trying to get me to cum first; naw, not today!

Pumping harder and longer strokes, I teased her clit again making it harder as I stuck my thumb in her ass; that did it. Devan let out a scream as she gushed all over my dick and I continued long stroking her. I grabbed her waist to help hold her up and dicked her like it was my last time ever getting the pussy. Seconds later I grunted, pulled out, and let my seed flush down the drain with the water.

Devan turned around, squatted, and sucked the rest of my nut out of me moaning and fondling my balls. I held onto the wall for strength. I grunted as she licked and slurped as I became semi-erect, but little man betrayed me, and I nutted in her mouth as she swallowed me whole stroking my balls. She stood up, winked at me, and grabbed the washcloth bathing me up as I did the same for her. After our shower, we sexed again in the bedroom, against the wall, and the floor. Spent, I pulled the comforter and sheets off the bed and wrapped us up, and that's where we slept until morning.

Chapter 25

Sara

I was glad the long weekend was over, and it was back to the work week. I was looking forward to seeing Erick again. I must admit, when I went home, I masturbated too many times off of his company's profile pic. I had even prank called him eleven times; just to hear his sexy ass husky voice. He sounded like R.L. from the hit group Nexxt. Yeah, I was petty betty, but I didn't give a fuck. I had even gone on Devan's Facebook page to lurk and see what they did that weekend. So, they went out on the town. To a museum, dinner, carriage ride around the park, shopping, and even to the improv to see Deray Davis. ARGH! I cannot stand that bitch. I mean I get that Erick doesn't like white women in that way, but he just hasn't run into this white woman. I was more than woman enough to give him what he needed. Hell, I could fuck him in any position too. I was a cheerleader in high school, I was just as flexible, and had just as much ass as Trish and Devan well, not Devan! Well, I was reduced to side lurking him. I had to find a way to get in his pants and fast! I would love a beautiful mixed brown baby by a fine, paid chocolate brother such as himself! Snapping out of my devious mind, I watched as Tyler stormed up the hallway and toward his desk. His damn face was all flushed and red, and he was sweaty; ew.

"Tyler, what gives bitch?" I asked.

"Gurl, Mr. Wallace just chewed my ass out!" he snapped.

"Bitch! Why? What the hell did you do this time?"

Tyler and I often got a little swat on our wrists for talking shit to our clients when they got attitude at times, or even for gossiping at work. Craig hasn't stepped to me or shot me an email. That was looking a little fishy on Tyler's part; no pun intended.

"Gurl, he was pissed because I mistakenly typed over a document and misspelled a few words, which I hardly ever do," he said dismissively, loud for passerbys and Devan to hear.

"Oh, damn", I said, "well you need to hurry up and fix that. Hell, I thought he was to call me next because we play a little on the job, you scared me cunt!" I laughed.

Tyler shooed me off with his hand as he grabbed paper towels fanning and wiping his face. I side glanced at him while tapping my pen for a few moments. He was acting funny, and it was bugging me. Not because he was back there for some time. I just felt he was hiding something from me.

I brushed off his weirdness and focused back on my task in front of me. I had to graph a thousand 'Thank You' letters from the company to Non-Profit Organizations that help people who suffer from Bipolar disorders. After some time, I stretched, downed the rest of my Frappe, and went to the bathroom to relieve myself. Checking myself in the mirror and applying more lip gloss, I heard the door open as Devan walked in. With a nod of her head, she passed me and went into the next available stall.

"Pssssssssst," I said as I twisted my lips and sucked my teeth.

This bitch thinks she is better than everybody because she's fucking the Boss. Well, I was fucking one too, just not the one I wanted. That will soon change, I hoped. Washing my hands again, I gave myself another once over and retreated to my station. As I sat down, I saw that Tyler was in a better mood as he rushed whomever it was off the phone.

"Who were you on the phone with?" I asked as I plopped down in my seat.

"Oh, nobody just Jason", he responded," he was asking if I wanted to check out the new gay bar that just opened on Bank Street called 'DIVAS.'"

"Oh, yeah I heard of that bar opening up, well hell, call him back and tell him, yes, and I'll come with," I said, " You know I'm your gay wife, and we always go together."

"Oookay then," Tyler said unenthusiastically.

Yeah, he is definitely hiding something, I thought to myself.

"Ok bitch, well whatever. Invite me or not invite me. I'm always your go-to bitch, but you seem to want to exclude me this time. It's cool," I said.

"Oh girl, you are so dramatic," Tyler laughed. "It's not that, I just wanted to hang with him and a new friend he wants me to meet, but I swear next time we go, you are coming with," he said trying to smooth over my feelings.

I was a little bit hurt because we always hang, but if he wanted an all 'boys' night, fine. I'll find something or hopefully someone to occupy me. I worked a few more hours until the huge Grandfather clock, that sat in the middle of the courtyard, rung five times, signaling my time to pack it up. I moved slowly just to see if Devan was going to stay later like she sometimes does or leave. If so, now will be my chance to have a go at Erick.

"Bye bitch', Tyler sang, as he gathered his belongings to leave.

"Bye yourself," I said as I gave him a half wave as he waltzed toward the elevators.

I busied myself cleaning around my desk, tying my trash bag up and setting it back down for the cleanup crew tonight. Ladies and Gents, as luck would have it, Devan was leaving out of her boo's office towards the elevators. I stuffed my wallet into my purse and grabbed my mug as if I was heading out as well. As the last of the staff headed out with Mr. Jones Sr, and Craig, I looked over my shoulder before going back into my bag and grabbed my medicine bag.

I unzipped it and looked over the few bottles of prescriptions I had to choose from. I didn't want him on anything too hard, so I just selected a minuscule cocktail of Ibuprofen, Tramadol, and Fluoxetine. Fluoxetine was for depression, and Tramadol a mild sedative for body pain. I gathered the pills, put them into a napkin, and put it in my bra. I zipped the bag of pills back up. Then put it in my bag under my desk. I know that Erick enjoyed an after-work cocktail in his office. Today I was going to administer him one with a side of a nice fat juicy pussy on the side!

Chapter 26

Sara

From where I was sitting, I could see Erick leaned back in his seat on the phone. I popped a fresh piece of gum in my mouth, adjusted my breasts, stood up, and sauntered over to his door. I tapped lightly and waited for him to wave me in. As I walked in, I closed the door and stood by the desk, and waited for him finish his call.

As he hung up, he focused his attention on me and asked, "Hey Sara what can I do for you?"

"Well, I started off, I'd like to pick your brain about something."

"Shoot," he said, as he leaned back and loosened his tie. Yes, that black on black Brooks Brother's suit and smokey gray Stacey Adam's he wore made him even more appealing, I thought as my pussy walls contracted, and I inadvertently bit my lower lip.

I caught myself in time and cleared my throat. "W-well, I um, see, Um, I wanted to move up the cooperate ladder, if you will, to chief secretary assistant. It has a better 401k plan, Dental, and I would be able to sign up for the Homeowners Insurance plan. I'm building a house from the ground up, and I want to have a more suitable job description that would be a career in the end." I looked at him as he stared through me pondering what I said.

"Well, Sara first, congrats on building your first home. That's awesome. I think that we can definitely help you in that area. Have you talked to Craig or my father about this?" he asked.

I stared at him meekly as I responded. "No, well, not officially. I wanted to ask you first to see if I could get with Nancy on the second floor. I want to make another intermediate opening application and background check, you know, a re-evaluation for the higher position."

"That wouldn't be hard at all. Of course, now a lot of companies are becoming stricter on their staff and up and coming, new employees. A mental evaluation, a more advanced background check, and of course their financial background, but of course if you pass that, then the next step isn't that much harder to do. You will be on your way. Are you up for that Sara? Are you well prepared?"

Hmmm, I could do that, if I had to rig up a mental eval. I could get my homegirl Grace down at M.H.C. -mental health center if need be.

"Hmm, yes, I think that I am capable of obtaining any and all documents needed for the next phase. Besides, I have been here a while, so that shouldn't be a problem, should it Erick?"

He looked up at me from his file drawer securing the packet to give me to start the process.

"No, I don't think so, but that being said Sara, there is that issue with your mental. I mean with you being Bipolar, and your depression... your therapist will have to sign off on your file. You have been seeing her on the regular, taking your medication on time, and every day so it should be ok. Also, you have to be on point and on task with your therapy. If there is any glitch or laps in your sessions, that will potentially hinder you from said position, or until your evaluation is up to par. That being said, have you gotten everything together to proceed with the interview?"

"Wow, you put a lot of information out there in a little bit of time, but yes I can get it all together for Nancy and be ready. Excuse me, Erick, please allow me to have a small drink? It's after six and I had gotten a bit overwhelmed at first, but I'm ok, now. May I fix you a drink as well," I asked him.

"Yes please, give me a shot of Hennessy on the rocks, while I run to the bathroom."

Perfect! I thought as I hurriedly took out the napkin with the medical cocktail and mixed it in as I poured his drink.

I opened the icebox, dropped three ice cubes, grabbed a straw and mixed the concoction. I placed his glass on his table and ran back to fix my drink all while trying not look flustered in the process. I blew out a breath as I sat my sneaky ass down just as Erick came out of the bathroom.

Fuck! That was close, I thought as I watched him gulp down his drink.

I jumped up and refilled his glass minus the drugs. Erick leaned back in his seat as he scrolled in his phone checking his emails. I noticed his eyes were getting a bit heavier as he blinked a few times and pinched the bridge of his nose. I smirked in my glass as I sipped on my drink.

Oh yes, OPERATION BIG DICK was now in progress!

Chapter 27

Erick

Man, I was not feeling good at all. I know it was a long day, and Devan was at home cooking dinner for us. I was anxious to get out of there when Sara stopped me from leaving. She was picking my brain for a newer, higher position in the firm that would solidify a permanent position as Chief Secretary. It would put Devan under Sara as her boss, but my girl was a trooper, and classy, Shit like that didn't phase her. Besides, she was going to move up in rank and work the floor above us, in which I was proud none the less. I blinked a few times as I looked up. I swore I saw Sara smiling at me.

Sara.. oh fuck!' I thought. If this was a setup with her doing something to me, I was going to be pissed.

"Are you done so that we can leave here?" I asked. "Roberto and his crew will be here to clean up, and I am ready to go," I drawled out.

My focus was started to fail me. I saw mini stars. My head felt as if an anvil fell from the sky and hit me. I was tired, very tired as I leaned back in my seat.

"Shhh, let mama take care of you," I heard as I tried to regain my focus.

"No, no, no," I slurred as a voice that was not my own sang out.

Sara's face came into view as I pushed her away. I assumed I pushed her away from me. My body was not cooperating with me as I felt her unzip my pants and start sucking on my tool. As much as I wanted and needed for her to stop, it felt good as fuck. I was so nervous. I felt like I failed Devan, but anyone can see I was sedated, right? I heard myself moan as Sara sucked me fast, then slow. She was gurgling and spitting on my dick as if it was a last meal and she wasn't sharing.

"Fuck, aw naw, fuck!" I thought as I bucked in my seat.

Sara grabbed my thighs to hold me in place which wasn't very hard because at this point I was useless. She was using me to her advantage and winning at this point. I struggled to move or at least push her away from me. She laughed at my weak ass attempt to get rid her. I was getting tired from lack of energy. I felt my dick get extra hard. I was trying to fight not to nut, but this chick was sucking me into oblivion, and I wasn't strong enough to manhandle her.

"Mmmmm, oh yes Erick. Yes, daddy nut in my mouth!" she moaned as I moaned.

"Devan, Devan he-help me, please!" That was all I could get out as my toes curled and my seed spilled out of me and down Sara's throat.

"Mmmm, yes, damn baby, that was good!" Sara said as she stood up and wiped her mouth.

She let out a roar of a laugh as she watched me slumped in my seat, breathing hard.

"Oh, I'm not done with you just yet," she said as she stroked me to an erection.

This bitch really thought she was going to fuck me, and *raw?!*

Oh, hell fuck naw!

I mustered some strength and pushed my chair back as she came towards me laughing.

"You are so fucking weak, what can you do?" she asked as she snorted.

"You are really crazy, really crazy, get the fuck away from me, now!" I barked at her.

My slurred, yelling fell on deaf ears as Sara hiked up her skirt and proceeded to put the tip of my dick in her. I didn't want to, but I used my strength as best as possible. I gut-punched this bitch. She yelped out as she flew across the room to landed on the couch. I jumped up trying to run but ended up on the ground.

I Hit my head on the edge of the desk and fell through the coffee table as it crossed, cutting me across my face, arms, and legs. I felt my ribs crack. I was at a loss for breath. My pants were around my ankles as I yelled for help. I yelled at the top of my lungs as I felt dizzy and began to see stars. Roberto ran in as Sara pushed passed him and ran out.

"Ple-please help me. She drugged me, please!" I said as I blacked out.

Chapter 28

Devan

After leaving work, I rushed home to shower and get dinner ready. It was date night and Erick, and I needed to catch up some much needed R&R. Throwing on a black cami and some PINK boy shorts, I set out to prepare dinner. About two hours later, I plated some pot roast with carrots, onions, and potatoes with yellow rice, rolls, and cabbage with ham. I was beat. I covered all the food and our plates and set them on the table with the unlit candles. I set Pandora on JOE's track and turned the volume down a bit. Yawning, I grabbed a blanket out of the closet and laid on the couch. I figured I'd catch some sleep as I waited for Erick to come in. I jumped up to sounds of someone banging on my front door.

"I'm coming hold up!" I shouted as I threw on a robe and checked the peephole.

Tyler was on the other side all frantic and crying. I snatched open the door and pulled him in.

"What the hell happened Ty, are you ok?" I asked as I searched his body for any visible marks, holes and or gunshots.

This was Detroit. You have to be careful. He was crying so loudly I couldn't make out what he was saying. I instructed him to calm down as he struggled to breathe. I wasn't prepared for what came out of his mouth next.

"It's Erick, h- he"

"WHAT Tyler!" I shouted

"Erick is hurt. I -I mean he is at Baptist Memorial Hospital. From what I heard, Sara drugged him and seduced him in his office. Then he passed out. You have to come."

As he said that, I dashed down the hall grabbing a pair of sweats out of the drawer and a hoodie. I threw on my sneakers, grabbed my purse and keys, and ran back up front. Tyler had turned off the radio and the stove as we ran out of the apartment. My nerves were so frazzled, and tears clouded my vision as I felt Tyler snatch my keys and lock the door. We made it outside to the Uber that was double parked. As Tyler gave the driver the address to the hospital, thoughts ran through my head. Were all the signs there about Sara? What would make her do this to him, to us? How did she drug him? I prayed and cried the entire ride as Tyler hugged me and consoled me. As we pulled up to the hospital, my legs suddenly felt like rubber, and I couldn't walk. Tyler helped me inside and to the front desk where he asked for the family of Erick Jones. I looked up as Mr. Jones Sr. and Mr. Wallace got our attention.

I ran up to them demanding questions.

"Is he ok? How is he? Where is he?"

Mr. Jones lovingly touched my shoulder calming me down and told me Erick was ok, and he was given tar to help him throw up. I felt my shoulders sink as fresh tears poured out of my eyes. Mr. Jones looked up and tapped my shoulders as the doctor came through the double doors toward us. I held my breath as I prepared for some unbearable news.

"Good, evening folks, I'm Doctor Benjamin Harris, and I'm the attending physician for Mr. Jones."

We all shook his hand as he continued to talk.

"When can we see him, Dr. Harris?" I asked.

Dr. Harris cleared his throat and began speaking again.

"Well, first let me just tell you that Mr. Jones has a slight concussion due to his fall. He has some lacerations to his face, arms, and hands, which we bandaged up. We also had to administer a flavored tar substance to get him help him regurgitate, but all is well, and he is expected to make a full recovery," he said. "You all can see him now, but please, two at a time and visiting hours will be over in 30 minutes.

"Thank you so much, Doctor Harris!" I exclaimed as I shook his hand.

He nodded his head and walked away to see another patient down the hall. Mr. Jones assured me that Erick was a trooper and he was going to be fine. He said, according to his son, Erick was about to lock up for the night and leave, after him and his father finished a debriefing over the phone when the incident happened. He also stated that Sara was behind this; as that much I knew, I got that info from Tyler on the way there.

Erick was in room 357A, and was in stable condition. The nurse came out to escort us to Erick's room. She also reminded us of the limited visiting hours and left us to see him. As we got into the room, the beeping of the monitor made me feel ill to my stomach. I looked at Erick laid up as he rested. I breathed a sigh of relief as I bent down to kiss him. He opened his eyes and smiled up at me.

"Hey"

"Hey, yourself."

"How do you feel?"

"I'm doing better. Sh-she really did a number on me. I'm sorry bae, I didn't slee-

"Baby, I know, I know you wouldn't do that to me, and I don't hold anything against you. We will talk about this when you out of here. This place creeps me out," I said as he grinned at me. "I'm going to be here when you wake up, and you will come home with me so I can play nurse and help heal you," I smirked as I leaned down to kiss him.

I grabbed a blanket and sank my body into the chair as I watched Tyler, Mr. Wallace, and Mr. Jones Sr. say their goodbyes and get well soons. Erick thanked all of them as he looked over at me and winked his eye.

"Devan, I love you, and I'm glad you are in my life."

My heart and stomach fluttered as I looked at this man that came into my world. Who knew a work crush would grow into something substantial? I remember damn near wanting to resign and work elsewhere to be far from him, afraid of rejection, and how he would feel about me. I felt like a High school girl who was crushing on the school's top sports jock, and afraid he wouldn't think twice to look in my direction. I was wrong, way wrong! I had a gorgeous loving, man by side who also went through much hell and trepidation with a crazed ex that wouldn't take no for an answer when he practically gave her the world! Well, that said man was giving me the world and was loving me all the same, and that completely humbled me and blessed me in a million ways! So, as I stared at him through tear-stained eyes, I uttered those same three words back at him.

"And I love you too, Erick."

Two months later...

Erick and I were doing much better. We are out of all of the drama and proceeded with our relationship. I was in bliss. Erick was doing a lot better after the encounter with Sara. He was back to work after taking a few weeks off. I got the promotion that I was looking at, which meant I was going to be working a floor up from him, but that didn't stop him from coming up to have "lunch" with me, or send flowers to my desk personally.

I was glad not to work so near to him, that way when he came over, or I went to his house, we kept our spice alive and were very much creative when we had sex. I was willing to do some things, we were looking to buy a sex swing that weekend. I couldn't wait to try it out.

I can say that I was sorry for how Trish ended up. As a woman scorned, we go through things that we either A) Allow ourselves to go through, or B) Take ourselves through it. Trish left Erick. Trish was unhappy in a happy relationship with Erick. I guess when you are given the world and don't have to work for it, you lose yourself and become selfish, whereas if you work for it, you know the sacrifices it took to get you there, so you cherish even the most simple thing possible.

Tyler still had his job, he was now head of the secretarial chair and is training two new employees to take my and Sara's positions. Good for him. He also is still seeing Mr. Wallace. I guess it's all the way out of the bag. I feel bad about Sara's demise. She was an evil bitch, but her death was gruesome. She was mentally bothered and shouldn't have been working at the firm. It didn't surprise us to get the word that she had died of a drug overdose, only to be found in her apartment a week later.

As for me, I'm glad that I gave Erick a chance. Hell, I gave myself a chance, a chance at love and some awesome ass sex with that fine ass Adonis god. He really is a stand-up guy looking to spoil a woman with love, sex, his money, time, and mostly affection. Who says nice girls can't finish first???

THE END...

WORKING ME OVERTIME

Looking for a publishing home?

After Hours Publications, is accepting submissions for writers in the Interracial Romance genre that excel in Paranormal, Contemporary, and Erotica. If you're interested, submit the first 3-4 chapters with your synopsis to Submissions@afterhourspublications.com.

Check out our website for more information: www.afterhourspublications.com.

Be sure to LIKE our After Hours Publications page on Facebook.

CPSIA information can be obtained
at www.ICGtesting.com
Printed in the USA
LVHW04s1543280518
578747LV00013B/1346/P